"If I ever marry, I need a woman who's going to challenge me in ways I've never been challenged. A woman who wants me to walk beside her as we go through life, but is independent and filled with vigor and passion."

He was so close that all Becca had to do was turn her head and their lips would be centimeters apart. Her heart was beating so fast that she couldn't hear anything else. She chanced a glance in his direction and was taken aback by the look she saw in his eyes.

"For this night to be about business," she said, "we sure are talking about a lot of nonbusiness-related topics."

"Is this just about business?" Josh asked. "Because this feels like a lot more than just business."

She turned to him then, filled with questions that she refused to ask and answers he'd never give. *Don't get lost in those baby blues.* She wasn't sure if it was the moonlight hitting his profile perfectly or the sound of the waves crashing on the shore in the distance, but the energy around them became even more electric.

"If we take this any further, it would be wrong."

"I disagree, Ms. Wright." Josh's eyes bounced from her eyes to her lips. "I think stopping here would be the real tragedy."

Dear Reader,

Although well-off, successful characters are a trademark of mine, millionaires were a new venture. I was drawn to a world of opposites in which two people start off in completely different places in life and cross unspoken boundaries, landing them exactly where they were destined to be.

Bad-boy millionaire Joshua DeLong may appear to be self-centered, but he earned his money and lifestyle through hard work while also breaking the rules along the way—a devilish trait that left him vulnerable to the dynamic and limitless Becca Wright. Becca's a destined debutante who left her lavish life behind to achieve more rewarding goals. She knows Josh's type, which means she'll do anything to ignore their chemistry…

I laughed out loud while writing Josh and Becca's story. My obsession with the little flaws that make people wonderful and perfect for one another made writing this book enjoyable and entertaining. Hope you enjoy it!

Much love,

Sherelle

authorsherellegreen@gmail.com

@sherellegreen

A Miami Affair

Sherelle Green

HARLEQUIN® KIMANI™ ROMANCE

Recycling programs
for this product may
not exist in your area.

ISBN-13: 978-0-373-86507-9

A Miami Affair

Copyright © 2017 by Harlequin Books S.A.

Special thanks and acknowledgment are given to Sherelle Green
for her contribution to the Millionaire Moguls miniseries.

HARLEQUIN®

www.Harlequin.com

Printed in U.S.A.

Sherelle Green is a Chicago native with a dynamic imagination and a passion for reading and writing. She enjoys composing emotionally driven stories that are steamy, edgy and touch on real-life issues. Her overall goal is to create relatable and fierce heroines who are flawed just like the strong and sexy heroes who fight so hard to win their hearts. There's no such thing as a perfect person…but when you find that person who is perfect for you, the possibilities are endless. Nothing satisfies her more than writing stories filled with compelling love affairs, multifaceted characters and intriguing relationships.

Books by Sherelle Green

Harlequin Kimani Romance

To Auntie Mickey, an independent, amazing
and fun-loving woman whom I've always admired.
I'm not sure if you remember this, but I recall that one
of the first books I ever got as a little girl came from
you. It was called *The Rainbabies*, and I read that book
so many times that the binding weakened. You always
understood my love for reading, and even as an adult,
you've supported me in all my endeavors. When asked
why I'm so creative, I often say it's because of you. Every
family has that one hidden treasure who passes down
traditions and values while ensuring that everyone
remains close-knit. For our family, you're that person,
and because of your generous and selfless spirit,
every single family member always feels like they have
you in their corner rooting them on. Saying thank you
doesn't seem strong enough to portray just
how much I appreciate having you in my life. You mean
so much to me and I am honored to be your niece.

Acknowledgments

To Auntie Val, a woman whose smile and laugh is
as infectious as her warm hugs. One of my fondest
memories is with you and Auntie Mickey on one of
our infamous shopping trips. I learned at a young age
that having aunts who I felt so close to was something
I would always cherish. One of the qualities that I've
always admired about you is your ability to teach a life
lesson in such a creative way that oftentimes your nieces
and nephews don't realize they've been taught a lesson
at all. You always give good advice, and it's obvious to
anyone that meets you that you keep your strong faith
and family values close to your heart. Thank you
so much for always being a sound voice in my life.
I feel so lucky to have you as my aunt.

Chapter 1

"**Y**ou've reached The Aunt Penny Foundation. Sorry, we are unable to take your call at the moment. Please leave your name, number and a detailed message, and we'll get back to you as soon as possible."

Joshua DeLong cringed at the sound of the annoying beep indicating that he had to leave yet another message for Becca Wright, the director of public relations for The Aunt Penny Foundation. It was even more frustrating that he didn't have Ms. Wright's direct cell phone number, forcing him to call the main line. Just as he was about to leave a voice mail, he got another call.

"At least someone is calling me back today," he said right before he switched to the incoming call. The call went precisely how he wished most of his business calls would go. Brief and in his favor.

Josh welcomed the light breeze that twirled through

his curly cocoa-colored hair. It was the perfect Miami June morning to spend outside on the upper deck of his luxury yacht that was more of a home to him than his condos in New York and LA. Maybe he preferred his yacht more than his other homes because it was the only one that offered the opportunity to escape reality whenever he wanted to. It's not that Josh normally needed a break from his everyday life, but lately he hadn't found solace living in any place that wasn't gently rocking from the waves made by boats leaving the private South Beach marina.

Josh placed his iPhone on the polished teak table and picked up his iPad while scoffing at his sunny-side up eggs and crisp turkey bacon. A quick glance at the time indicated that the morning was already getting away from him. He needed to leave for LA in the afternoon, so he had to be productive this morning. Unfortunately, Ms. Wright played an important part in that. Last night, he'd emailed a couple contacts to see if they could get ahold of Ms. Wright's personal cell number, but he hadn't heard back yet.

He scrolled through the articles about The Aunt Penny Foundation he'd bookmarked yesterday and began reading where he'd left off last night. It was an interview with Becca Wright and the founder of the organization, Haley Adams. Although both women had impressive résumés, it was Becca's that had caught his eye. Ivy League graduate with years of charity and fundraising experience. Accomplished violinist. A host of academic accolades. Given what he'd briefly read about Becca in two other articles, he wasn't surprised by those details.

A calendar reminder popped up on his iPad prompting him to call his friend and fellow Prescott George member Daniel Cobb. Josh remembered a time when he'd been building his brand as a corporate raider, hoping for an exclusive invitation to join Prescott George— or the Millionaire Moguls as they were informally known—a prestigious, all-male national organization that was as powerful as it was discreet. However, he'd always assumed it was wishful thinking. Prescott George didn't invite just anyone to join, especially a man of his caliber, who was considered a nouveau riche tycoon instead of an old-money legend. The latter were handed invitations into the organization based on their last names or historic financial statuses. When he'd finally gotten invited, by another member of the nouveau riche, he'd jumped at the opportunity to join Prescott George.

Staring at the calendar reminder once more, Josh reset the notification to have it ping him in another hour. He scrolled a little further through the article he was reading until he landed on a picture of Becca Wright. She was wearing a white collared shirt buttoned to the neck underneath a black suit jacket that appeared two sizes too big for her. Either that or she just had broad shoulders. He couldn't tell.

Josh opened another tab on his iPad to Google images of Becca. More pictures appeared, each one more conservative than the next. One photo made him pause. In it Becca was wearing a beige cardigan over a plain white top. Her hair was pulled atop her head in a tight bun and her large black-rimmed glasses were a tad too big for her oval face. She was wearing little makeup and although she was smiling, her smile didn't reach her eyes. *Have I seen her somewhere before?* There was something vaguely familiar about her photo, but he couldn't quite place it.

Grabbing his phone, he decided to call the foundation once more and leave another voice mail. Once again, he was greeted by the beep.

"Hello, this is Joshua DeLong from Prescott George calling for Ms. Wright, *again.* As you know, The Aunt Penny Foundation has been chosen as the charity beneficiary for our annual fundraising gala this summer. As I stated in my previous voice mail, I have to go out of town this afternoon and therefore…" His voice trailed off as he realized why Becca looked so familiar. She looked exactly like Ms. Perkins. His horrible middle school principal. Although according to his research Becca was only twenty-eight years old, Josh had no doubt that his middle school principal—who was much older than Becca—had been dressed in the exact same shirt and cardigan, with the exact same hairdo and glasses, for one of their school pictures decades ago.

"We need to meet this morning," Josh said, abruptly ending the call. He had definitely planned on leaving his cell phone number and a couple other details in his voice mail, but he hadn't been able to shake the feeling that Becca reminded him of the woman whose office was still etched in his memory, since Josh had always found himself in some type of trouble.

He obviously knew that he hadn't been leaving a voice mail for Ms. Perkins, but the minute the realization had hit him, he hadn't been able to shake the feeling. Ms. Perkins was probably the meanest woman he'd ever met in his life, and that was saying a lot since Josh had met his fair share of unpleasant people.

"I couldn't stand that lady," he said aloud to no one

but himself. "She made my childhood hell." He shivered as he glanced at Becca's photo once more. He could only hope that he wasn't dealing with Ms. Perkins's clone.

"Ten, nine, eight, seven…" Becca Wright tried her best to calm her rattled nerves as she shuffled through stacks of unruly papers and file folders on her desk. "Six, five, four, three, two, one." She stopped what she was doing and took a deep breath. She'd been doing intervals of ten while trying to organize her desk for thirty minutes straight, then taking ten-second breaks in between.

Ever since the receptionist for The Aunt Penny Foundation suddenly quit last week, Becca had been under more stress than she'd ever been before. Usually she was great at multitasking and managing several projects simultaneously. However, the temporary receptionist that had arrived yesterday had spent more time chatting on the phone with her friends or stepping outside for cigarette breaks than actually doing the work she'd been hired to do.

"Stacy!" Becca yelled after her short break was over. "Where is the file for the incoming students who arrived yesterday?"

After several minutes, Stacy strolled around the corner, loudly smacking her gum. "Um, what do you expect from me? I just started a few days ago, so why would I know where it is?"

Becca rapidly blinked her eyes. *Teenagers today… I'd never talk to my boss like that.* "Well, yesterday your only project was to enter the information for the new students who just joined The Aunt Penny Foundation into our intranet. It was a simple job."

Stacy gave her a blank stare.

Becca waved her hands in frustration. "Never mind. Just tell me where you put my messages. I'm expecting an important call."

"Don't you have a cell phone?"

"Yes," Becca said through gritted teeth. "But not everyone has my cell phone number and it's your job to answer the phone. I haven't heard it ring off the hook for a while, so at least you're doing that."

"Oh no, I'm not." Stacy flipped her long black hair over her shoulder. "I took it off the hook because I couldn't hear my phone call over the loud ringing. A Jonathan Delaney kept calling."

Becca went through a mental checklist of important calls she was expecting and couldn't recall that name. Nor did she find it in her Rolodex.

"You know," Stacy continued, "you should think about getting rid of the landline and only using your cell phone. No one uses landlines anymore. They don't keep business cards, either. Everything is online now."

Unbelievable. "I'm surprised you even know what a landline is." Normally, Becca would have had some more choice words for the young woman, but for now, she just needed to check her calls. Haley was working offsite with a few students, which meant Becca had a lot to accomplish with zero help from the useless temp. She wanted to confirm her appointment tomorrow with the Prescott George representative she was scheduled to meet. What was his name again? She scrunched her forehead and snapped her fingers when it came to her. Joshua DeLong.

"Oh no," Becca said as she rushed out of her office to the main desk. *What are the odds that Jonathan Del-*

aney is actually Joshua DeLong? She hoped her in-kling was wrong, but given her week so far, she feared he was the one who'd called before Stacy had taken the phone off the hook.

The front desk was even more unorganized than hers was. She moved Stacy's oversize book bag from the desk. After a little more digging, she finally found the phone and was able to listen to the messages. She skipped a few until she heard the deep, silky voice of a man who introduced himself as Joshua DeLong. He'd called twice and the last abrupt voice mail he'd left was from an hour ago.

"Stacy!" Becca yelled again. And yet again, Stacy took her sweet time strolling to the front desk. "Don't you remember me mentioning yesterday that I was ex-pecting an important call from Joshua DeLong? Did you even stop to think that maybe you heard his name wrong when he called?"

"Oh, that explains it," Stacy said, nodding her head. "He sounded even more annoyed during his last voice mail."

"You listened to his messages and didn't tell me?"

Instead of responding, Stacy just shrugged and walked away. Becca jotted down the number Joshua left and called him back.

"Hello, this is Joshua DeLong."

"Mr. DeLong, it's Becca Wright with The Aunt Penny Foundation. I want to apologize for not receiv-ing your voice mails until now."

"It's quite all right. I still have a couple hours be-fore I have to go to the airport. Can you meet today?"

"Sure, just name the place and time." Meeting Mr. DeLong today as opposed to tomorrow was a bit of an inconvenience, but the foundation needed the assistance of Prescott George so rearranging her schedule was a necessity.

"So I'm meeting you at the Southern Royal Yacht Club in South Beach?" Becca was a little taken aback by the location. One had to be a member to even enter the gate of the high-class boutique marina. Members included the rich, famous and elite.

"Yes. I'll meet you at the clubhouse gate entrance. And in case you have any apprehensions, rest assured that you'll be fine. We Royal yachtees get a bad rep since we're so exclusive, but we're just regular people."

Yeah, right. "Okay, not a problem. I can be there in forty minutes." She ended the call a little less frazzled than she'd been before. She was sure Mr. DeLong was unaware of her upbringing since she rarely discussed her family's social or financial status in interviews. However, she knew *exactly* what type of members frequented the Southern Royal Yacht Club and *regular* was not the word she would use to describe them.

"Oh, he is hot."

Becca turned at the sound of Stacy's voice. "What did you say?"

Stacy tapped her phone a few more times before walking over to Becca. "Have you seen the photos online of Joshua DeLong? I Googled him while you were on the phone."

"You can't do any work, but you can eavesdrop on my calls?"

Stacy didn't respond, but instead passed her phone to Becca. *Mercy.* His deep blue eyes were the first feature she noticed. They were striking against his toasted-caramel complexion and curly cocoa-brown hair.

"Hot, right?" Stacy asked. Becca stared at the photo a little longer before passing Stacy back her phone.

"Listen, I have to meet Mr. DeLong and I don't trust you to be here by yourself, so I'm locking up the office. Why don't you just come back tomorrow."

"I still get paid for today, right?"

Becca glared at Stacy. *Note to self: call the temp agency after my meeting with Mr. DeLong.*

"Stacy, just pack your things so I can lock up." Becca needed to be fresh and alert for her meeting with Mr. DeLong and the only good thing Stacy had done since arriving was showing her that photo.

On the drive to the marina, Becca recalled everything she'd read about Joshua DeLong. Thirty-five. Never been married. No kids. Recently named one of the most influential black men in America. Built his fortune from the ground up as a corporate raider. Despite his accomplishments, she also recalled another article that named him one of the most ruthless men in America. Judging by what she knew about corporate raiders, she had to agree with some of the statements in the second article. Building your career on the misfortune of others was hardly admirable. Especially since Becca had spent the majority of her life on the opposite end of the spectrum by trying to provide fortune to the misfortunate.

As she neared the yacht club, she noticed a tall male figure standing just outside the main gate wearing basketball shorts and a white tee. Hardly the outfit one would wear for a business meeting.

She parked her car in an open spot and made her way to Joshua DeLong. The closer she got, the more nervous she got. *Oh, come on, Becca, you've seen at-*

tractive men before. She couldn't even make out all of his facial features since he was wearing Ray-Bans and a baseball cap, but just the way he was standing was enough to make her take notice. His posture was confident. Self-assured. He may have looked casual in his clothing, but his aura seemed anything but.

"Hello, I'm Becca Wright," she said as she approached. "It's nice to meet you in person, Mr. DeLong."

"Please, call me Joshua or Josh." He extended his hand.

"Only if you call me Becca." She accepted his warm handshake and was rewarded by a smile that displayed a brilliant set of white teeth.

"Please follow me, Becca." Becca had assumed they were meeting inside the clubhouse, until Josh walked past the building and began leading her down a ramp toward the boats.

"Where are we going?" she asked after several minutes.

"To my yacht."

She quirked an eyebrow even though he couldn't see her. "Your yacht? As in your own private yacht?"

His head slightly turned over his shoulder in her direction. "Yes, my own private yacht."

She frowned. "Wouldn't it be better if we conducted business in a more public place like the clubhouse?"

"No." Josh continued to walk, offering her no additional explanation.

"No? That's it?"

She was so busy trying to keep up with him, she hadn't noticed that he'd slowed his stride. "We're here." He motioned for her to walk up a ramp that led to a beautiful three-story white yacht. There wasn't much that left Becca speechless, but the sight before her hijacked her words. The yacht was grand and one of the larger vessels in the marina.

When she arrived on the first level, she noticed two packets placed on a sleek wooden table.

"Please, have a seat," Josh said as he pointed to an L-shaped timber sofa with black cushions and white pillows.

She didn't hesitate to take a seat, secretly eager to feel if the cushions were as lush as they appeared. *Even more lush*, she thought, adjusting herself in her seat. Josh took a seat adjacent to her.

As Becca was relishing her comfort, Josh removed his baseball cap and ran his fingers through his brown curls. *I wonder if they're as soft as they look.*

"Okay, shall we get down to business?" Josh shuffled through some papers before he removed his Ray-Bans and glanced at her. *Oh my.* He smiled in a way that she assumed made women drop their panties instantly. Of course, she didn't feel the effects of his smile, but she could see how many women would.

"Yes, let's get started." She tried her best to focus on the packet in front of her instead of his stunning eyes. If Becca were the type to swoon over a pretty face, Joshua's would have had her in a puddle on the floor. Fortunately, she'd met plenty of handsome men who were gorgeous on the outside but ugly on the inside. The verdict was still out as to whether that described Joshua DeLong.

Chapter 2

Josh smiled as he watched Becca concentrate on the packet he'd given her. He got the feeling that she was the type to never act too affected by a man, but he hadn't missed the hint of appreciation reflected in her eyes.

"I apologize if you had to change any plans to see me today. As I stated over the phone, I wanted to meet before I head out of town. I have big plans for the benefit, but I want to make sure my ideas work for Aunt Penny."

"I guess I should explain the foundation in a little more detail," Becca said, turning toward Josh. "Unless you prefer to dive right into the plans."

"No, please continue. I'd like to hear more about the foundation."

"Well, as you know, I'm the director of public relations for The Aunt Penny Foundation, which was founded by Haley Adams. Haley and I aren't just colleagues, but friends who share the same vision. And while Aunt Penny is a real person, she doesn't actually work at the foundation or oversee its activities."

"But Aunt Penny contributes financially, right?" Josh asked. "I believe I read an article about her being a key sponsor for the foundation." Josh reached for the water bottles he'd placed on the table before Becca had arrived and offered her one.

"Thank you," she said, opening the water bottle and taking a sip. "Yes, Aunt Penny is definitely a key supporter and the reason the foundation exists in the first place. Aunt Penny was Haley's next-door neighbor when she was growing up and although Aunt Penny isn't actually Haley's blood relative, she became somewhat of a surrogate grandmother to her. Aunt Penny's emotional encouragement and financial support are the reason Haley earned an Ivy League diploma."

"Aunt Penny sounds pretty special." Josh hadn't had the benefit of meeting his paternal grandmother, but he imagined that she would have been like Aunt Penny. Unfortunately, he couldn't say the same for his mom's mother, who didn't have a nurturing bone in her body.

"She is." Becca nodded her head in agreement. "There will always be a special place for Aunt Penny in my heart, too. One day, Haley came to me and said that she wished every girl could have an Aunt Penny, and thus, the foundation was born. Our nonprofit organization helps students who otherwise couldn't afford it raise money for college. We provide mentoring, as well."

Josh knew what the foundation did and had researched them at length, but it was nice to hear the words from Becca directly. "That's a great story and one that I believe should be shared at our upcoming Prescott George meeting. The history of the foundation is also one that the media would truly love."

Becca squinted. "Haley and I would be happy to share the foundation's story with the organization, but I'm confused. I don't recall any of the previously chosen charity recipients receiving media coverage."

"That's because they haven't. But I've thought at length about your foundation and the increased number of donations you would receive if we invite celebrities to the gala. Celebrities will not only be willing to break out their checkbooks, but also speak with the media about the event and your organization."

Josh vaguely thought about the fact that the Prescott George board had yet to understand his vision for the gala. However, in due time he was hoping a few key members would begin to see things his way.

"I'm all for increased revenue, but I don't want The Aunt Penny Foundation to be subject to a paparazzi circus, either."

"More paparazzi mean more donations."

"I'm surprised this is the route Prescott George wants to take." She was studying him carefully, but Josh didn't care. He was confident that publicizing the gala was the right move and getting Becca to agree would only help him pitch his argument to the board.

"Sometimes, in order to get the larger population to donate to a cause, you've got to take risks."

"Sometimes the risk isn't worth the reward."

"And other times it is." Josh sat up straighter in his seat. "We have less than two months before the gala, so we need to act fast on a few of the ideas I have if we're going to solidify the appearance of celebrities."

Seeing the skepticism on her face, Josh thought she'd probably get along with Ashton extremely well. Both were afraid to take chances. Ashton Rollins was the current president of Prescott George and Josh had no doubt that Rollins would host operations out of a dark cave if he could. Ashton lived and breathed boring traditions and was never willing to take risks that could potentially benefit the organization.

Becca pushed her packet aside and turned her entire body toward Josh. "Would I be correct if I assumed you're one of those people who believe that there is no such thing as bad publicity?"

"You'd be correct," Josh said with a smile. "As long as you're leading an honest life, you should have nothing to fear from the media. Photos and articles about me pop up on newsfeeds all the time. Something about me is constantly floating around on some form of media, whether it be false or true information. Yet, instead of letting what's portrayed define me, I use the media to my advantage. The publicity only fuels my success."

Becca was already shaking her head in disagreement. "I can't imagine every part of my life surfacing on newsfeeds. Especially if it's depicted in a negative or false manner. If I wanted to be in the media all the time, I would have taken up acting."

Josh laughed. "In today's connected world, you have to be willing to put yourself out there. In regards to the gala, we would control media coverage as opposed to the media controlling us."

"I understand your point, but I'd much rather be known for what I accomplish, and based on coverage I've seen where celebrities attend fundraisers, it's more about who they may be dating or what they're wearing rather than the cause."

A quick glance at the time let him know that he needed to wrap up the meeting. He should have ended it ten minutes prior, yet strangely enough, he was enjoying his debate with Becca too much to end the conversation there.

"Becca, I can promise you that Prescott George has The Aunt Penny Foundation's best interests in mind." He leaned a little closer to her. "What you and Haley are doing for less fortunate students is admirable and I appreciate the vision and history behind your organization. I only want to help others see the amazing work you're doing. You don't just have the support of Prescott George for the gala. You have our support in all your efforts for the future.

"If you allow me to implement some of my publicity ideas for your foundation, I promise that you will not be disappointed. So what do you say? Are you on board?"

For a few seconds, he wondered if she'd been listening to what he'd said. She was looking directly at him, but her mind seemed to be miles away. The silence gave him the chance to observe her a little more closely. She looked a lot better in person than she did in her pictures.

"Okay," she finally said. "If you think that having the media present will result in additional donations for the foundation, then I'm willing to give it a try. I'm sure you have to leave for your flight soon, so I'll review the rest of the packet and discuss it with Haley before getting back to you."

"Sounds good. I'll also send you the information electronically before my flight." Josh extended his hand to her.

Becca glanced at his hand, but didn't shake it. "If I disagree with any of your ideas, then we'll rework the plan before you take action, right?"

"I'll agree to that."

"Good. Then we have a deal." She finally shook his hand and when she did, he briefly relished how soft it was.

After he led her off his yacht and back through the gate, he smiled as he watched her walk away. *You surprised me, Becca Wright.* He couldn't quite place his reasoning, but he had a feeling he'd just met his next big challenge.

Becca glanced at the clock on the wall. 9:00 p.m. She should have left the office hours ago, but she still had a mountain of paperwork to enter into the intranet and loads of mail to organize before she could call it a night.

"I think I've zapped all my brain cells for one day," Haley said, standing near the doorway of Becca's office. "I think you should tackle the rest of your to-do list tomorrow."

Becca ran her fingers down her face. "I wish I could, but I forgot to call the temp agency about Stacy and I really want to get some more work done."

"I figured you'd say that." Haley walked to the front desk and came back with two cupcakes and two coffees.

"You read my mind," Becca said accepting her coffee and cupcake. "Is this from the new bakery down the street?"

"Sure is. I asked Leanna to get it for us before she left."

"For this, I can take a break." Becca cleared a small space on her desk as Haley took a seat across from her.

As usual, they were the last two in the office. In the span of one year, The Aunt Penny Foundation had gone from twelve dedicated employees to five, including Becca and Haley and the part-timers. In a way, Becca couldn't even blame their receptionist for abruptly quitting. To say that the foundation had seen better times would be an understatement.

Becca took a bite of the cupcake. "Oh my God, this tastes so good."

"It does," Haley agreed. "Gooey red velvet goodness. The perfect carbs for a long day. Which reminds me… The temp, Stacy, showed me a picture of Joshua DeLong this morning. Does he look as sexy in person as he does in the photos online?"

Becca frowned. "We can't get the temp to do actual work, but she shows off Josh's picture with the same amount of dedication that we wished she'd put into her job?"

"Oh, so you're already on a first-name basis with the Millionaire Mogul?"

Becca laughed. It was a well-known fact that the Prescott George organization was often referred to as the Millionaire Moguls. "Have you read the articles online about Josh?"

"Of course I have." Haley took a sip of her coffee. "Stacy was eager to have me read a couple articles, as well."

"Tomorrow I'm calling the temp agency for sure," Becca said, shaking her head. "Anyway, most of the articles portray him as a cocky, arrogant corporate raider who can somehow ease the worries of even the most skeptical client. Those qualities—combined with his charm—are what make him a force to be reckoned with."

"Did you get a different impression?" Haley asked. "Was he less impressive than what the articles say?"

Becca thought about the meeting she'd had with Josh, from the moment she introduced herself to him all the way to the moment he walked her back to the gate. "I wouldn't exactly call the articles false."

Haley raised an eyebrow. "Okay, bestie, what aren't you telling me?"

Even now, Becca could feel those vibrant blue eyes watching her walk to her car. "He was exactly how one would imagine Joshua DeLong to be…cocky, arrogant and charming. He spent the majority of the meeting trying to convince me that inviting celebrities to the gala would give our foundation an opportunity to receive even more donations and offer unprecedented media coverage."

"That sounds awesome," Haley said enthusiastically. "I knew I had a good feeling about working with the moguls."

"You would be okay with all the publicity? What if all the media coverage doesn't truly capture the essence of The Aunt Penny Foundation?"

Haley shrugged. "Isn't it better to give ourselves the free publicity and take every chance we can to try to save the foundation?"

That was exactly what Josh had said. "If you're okay with it, then I'll email you the information he sent me so that you can review it, as well. I'll admit he has some pretty good ideas. I just want to make sure I understand his angle."

"I know that look," Haley said. "You don't trust him."

"I barely know him."

"Exactly. So you don't trust him?"

Becca thought about his perfect white teeth, soft-looking curly hair and grand yacht. "I'm just skeptical, and Josh is a smooth talker. By the end of our conversation, he *almost* had me convinced that I should just hand over the reins and let him drive the entire time."

Haley's eyes softened. "Listen, Becca, we both know that the past couple years have been difficult for the foundation. We aren't getting the sponsorships and donations we were before. Economically, we're facing a crisis, and you and I didn't both get Ivy League educations and quit our corporate jobs to see The Aunt Penny Foundation fail."

"We'll figure something out before it comes to that," Becca said as she reached across the table and touched Haley's hand. "Do you remember what we used to say in college?"

Haley smiled. "'At the end of the day, there's always chocolate and coffee'?"

Becca laughed. "Not that one. I was thinking about when we used to say that one day, we were going to accomplish something that would change the lives of others."

"Of course I remember. In college, we were bright-eyed and ready to conquer the world."

"And now we're doing just that. After only a few years, we've already helped over one hundred students get full scholarships to colleges and universities. That's not even including partial scholarships. We're making a difference every day at The Aunt Penny Foundation and we will continue to do so for years to come."

"Then try to keep an open mind when it comes to

Joshua DeLong," Haley said. "Regardless of how you feel about him, keep your mind on the prize. I know how skeptical you are with men like him, but now is not the time to let your prejudices cloud your judgment. We need this, Becks."

Whenever Haley used her nickname, Becca knew Haley was nervous or anxious about a situation. In this case, it was in Becca's best interest to take her friend's advice and focus on all the good that would come from being Prescott George's charity recipient.

"Don't worry, Haley. We have the opportunity of a lifetime right in front of us and I have every intention on The Aunt Penny Foundation reaping as many benefits as we can."

Even if I have to work with a man like Joshua De-Long.

Chapter 3

"It's about time," Josh said as he crashed onto the long black sofa in the living room of his condo. He'd been in LA for a couple days, in back-to-back meetings with the shareholders of the latest corporation he'd invested in. Last night, he thought they'd finally reached an agreement, just to be sucked into an even longer debate.

The last time he'd been in several consecutive all-day and all-night meetings that concluded with little solution to the problem had been during the early stages of his career. Josh was usually better at conducting his business meetings, but this tech company wasn't as agreeable as he'd hoped. Times like this really made his job difficult. Josh didn't have any misconceptions about the type of work he was in, but in some ways, it still took a toll on him when he least expected it.

Since his meetings had run longer than expected,

he'd also missed a call from Daniel Cobb, a Millionaire Mogul he'd been playing phone tag with. He really needed to set up a time to see Daniel in person. Their discussion about the current state of Prescott George couldn't wait any longer.

Lately thinking about the organization left a bad taste in his mouth. As the Moguls grew across the nation, so did their rigid and old-school values that didn't allow for much growth within the organization. According to the unspoken rule, a man like Josh would never be chosen as president of the organization. Current president Ashton Rollins—or Mr. Bland and Boring, as Josh secretly referred to him—was just another example of birthright rising to the top. The same affluent families holding the positions of power, subjecting the Prescott George members to the same snooze-fest that was guaranteed to keep the organization stagnant. Josh was ready to change all that.

It was no secret that Josh wasn't the typical PG member. While most of the men followed the strict dress code and proper forms of speech when attending their meetings, Josh was the complete opposite. He wore what he wanted, how he wanted. Said what he wanted, when he wanted. His actions made many members feel as if he didn't belong. However, Josh was learning that there were quite a few members who were just as fed up with the status quo as he was. Including Daniel Cobb.

It was past time for PG to have some new blood running the organization. Even though Josh was unhappy with their traditional values, he was still proud to be a member of Prescott George. The Moguls continued to do good work by providing college scholarships to less-fortunate students and funding to inner-city organizations. Honoring an organization such as The Aunt Penny Foundation was just icing on the cake. Being in charge of charity outreach and public relations for PG meant that Josh was able to make an impactful difference in the lives of others.

The gala could be the turning point Prescott George needed. Not only that, but The Aunt Penny Foundation would reap the benefits. Josh knew that Becca was skeptical, but he had no doubt in his mind that gaining media coverage would bring the foundation to the next level.

Josh yawned and took a long stretch before turning on his side on the sofa. He was more restless than he had been in months. Ever since he was a kid, he'd experienced nervous energy. His parents had noticed that he'd often had a difficult time concentrating on one thing at a time, but had thought it was something he'd grow out of. Josh could still remember all the doctor's appointments when they were trying to diagnose him with attention deficit hyperactivity disorder. It had taken years for his teachers and parents to realize that he wasn't suffering from ADHD, but rather wasn't being challenged enough in school. His IQ was considerably higher than that of the average student his age and he was able to skip two grades.

Usually, Josh would call a woman he often contacted when he was in LA to see if she wanted to stop over and help ease his restlessness. Strangely enough, after a night like he'd had, there was only one person he wanted to see.

Without thinking about it, he pulled out his phone and began scrolling through the contacts on his Skype app until he found Becca's contact information. Being that it was early in the morning, he didn't expect her to answer, but surprisingly she did. And from the looks of it, she was wearing what he assumed was her normal work attire.

"Hello, Becca. I'm glad you answered."

"Hello, Josh." The way she'd said his name sounded a lot friendlier than the look she was currently giving him. "You didn't strike me as the type to give 4:00-a.m. wake-up calls. Is everything okay? Are you calling about the questions I had regarding the paperwork?"

Shoot. Josh had seen her email come through about twelve hours ago and had been unable to review her questions. Typically he wouldn't reach out to someone until he had answers for them.

"I'm sorry. I just got out of a consecutive forty-eight-hour meeting, so I haven't gotten a chance to look at the email you sent yet."

Becca leaned out of the screen and returned covering her mouth, obviously chewing. "I understand. Please excuse my chewing. I haven't eaten for hours and I just got home from work not too long ago. I haven't even been to sleep yet."

"Wow! I didn't know charity work could keep you up until the wee hours of the morning."

Becca frowned. "I guess in your world, Mr. DeLong, what I do is of little importance and couldn't possibly keep me up at this ungodly hour."

Ouch. He was usually a lot smoother with the ladies. "Once again, I find myself apologizing to you, Becca. I misspoke. It wasn't my intention to offend you. What I meant to say was that I'm curious about what you do at the foundation and I'd be interested in learning more. I can tell you're very dedicated."

"I am very dedicated, Mr. DeLong." Her mouth

clenched. "I'm intelligent too, so I know very well what you meant."

Josh didn't mean to laugh, but the way she was formally addressing him proved that in the course of twenty seconds he'd managed to piss her off. "I must say, Becca, it usually takes longer than a few seconds for me to rub someone the wrong way."

"I'm sure your charm may work on most. However, you can't insult me and then assume that an apology will make me forget those words ever came out of your mouth."

"Jeez," Josh said, still laughing. "Tough crowd."

He watched the line in her forehead indent even more than it had seconds prior. Although she was annoyed with him, there was something cute about the way her nose crinkled when she frowned.

"Maybe I'm overreacting a little."

Josh raised an eyebrow. "Just a little?"

"It's been a long day, so I'll just blame my mood on lack of sleep."

"No worries. I should have thought about what I said before I said it. But as you stated, it's been a long day."

"Speaking of a long day, I was about to finish my food and go to bed. Is there anything I can help you with beforehand?"

Josh usually thought quickly on his feet, but there was something about Becca that made him pause and really think about the words he said next. "I don't mind if you eat while we chat. I didn't want to speak to you about anything in particular."

She looked skeptical, but took another bite of her food. Josh liked the way her mouth moved. She was a slow chewer, which made the movement of her mouth downright hypnotizing.

"I'm being honest. I called you because I was exhausted, and for some reason you're the only person I wanted to talk to. So if you need to hang up, it's fine."

If they hadn't been on Skype, he wouldn't have gotten a chance to see her almond-shaped eyes widen and her lips slightly open in surprise.

For a couple minutes, neither of them said anything. Josh welcomed the silence and took the moment to observe Becca more closely; she appeared to be observing him, as well. Staring into a woman's eyes for more than a minute—especially one whom he'd just met—wasn't a regular occurrence for Josh. As cocky as it sounded, when he set his sights on a woman, looking deeply into each other's eyes for an extended period of time wasn't a part of the deal. It tended to send women the wrong message and then they got attached too quickly. Yet Josh felt as though he could look into Becca's light brown eyes all night.

Even though she was fatigued, her warm golden-mocha complexion glowed under the dim lighting of what he assumed was her bedroom. He could only see the edge of a white pillow propped behind her back and the corner of what appeared to be a nightstand where her plate of food was sitting. When Becca adjusted herself, displaying a little more of her clothing, Josh forgot about the pillow as his eyes dropped to her blouse, which was slightly open.

It wasn't gentlemanlike to look down a woman's shirt, but in his defense he hadn't expected the top two buttons to be undone. He'd expected her blouse to be buttoned all the way to the neck, the way it had been in all the photos he'd seen of her.

He must have been staring too long, because Becca glanced down at her shirt and then proceeded to cover up her chest as if she was exposing too much skin. Josh hadn't even seen a hint of cleavage, but he assumed it was still more than Becca wanted him to see. When she met his eyes, she shook her head at him.

"What?" he asked, feigning innocence.

"Nothing," she said, taking another bite of her food. This time when she chewed, her food must have gone down the wrong pipe because it sent her into a coughing frenzy.

"Are you okay?" he asked.

"I'm okay," she said, still coughing. "Sometimes, when I put something large in my mouth too fast, I choke. I should have done it slower."

Does she have any idea how sexual that sounded? Amusement must have shown on his face because she choked even more.

"That came out wrong."

"No, I think it came out right."

"I didn't mean to say that I'm always putting big things in my mouth. I meant to say that sometimes my throat has to get adjusted before I swallow." Becca gasped and quickly covered her mouth, but it was too late. Josh had already heard her and was unsuccessful at stifling his laughter.

"Okay, that came out wrong, too." Becca placed her hands in front of her as if she were bracing herself before she continued speaking. "I've had issues with gagging if I don't properly prepare myself."

Josh chuckled even more than he had before. On one

hand, he was actually surprised that there was reasoning behind why she was chewing so slowly. He should have asked her to explain to indicate that he was indeed listening. Yet the situation was much too amusing.

"This is by far the most amusing conversation I've had all day, Becca." He wiped a few tears that were forming in the corners of his eyes from laughing so hard. "Thanks for the laugh. I needed that."

"I'm here all week." Her smile was tight-lipped, causing him to laugh as hard as he had before. Eventually, she started laughing along with him. Josh liked the sound of her laughter. Instead of being high-pitched like he'd assumed it would be, her laugh was smooth as velvet.

They talked for a few more minutes before disconnecting their call. Josh didn't bother to get up and head to his bedroom. Instead, he spent the next twenty minutes thinking about Becca before he drifted off to sleep on the sofa. He'd worry about why the buttoned-up PR director was on his mind later.

Chapter 4

"Please tell me that you didn't tell one of the sexiest men in Miami that you had a gag reflex problem?"

Becca looked up from her desk at Leanna Timmons—part-time program manager for The Aunt Penny Foundation. Leanna had been the first employee to join the foundation and had been an asset to Haley and Becca over the years. Leanna also owned her own hair and beauty salon down the street from the office. Today, her blond hair was cut in a chic bob and highlighted with pink and black streaks that matched her black tank and pink skirt. On any other person, the style might have looked crazy, but on Leanna it made her look like a rock star.

"That's not how the conversation went."

Leanna crossed her arms over her chest. "Oh really? When I talked to Haley this morning, she said you basically admitted that you suffer from a sensitive gag reflex when something large goes into your mouth."

Becca sighed. She'd told Haley not to mention what had happened, but apparently her best friend hadn't listened. She couldn't even chastise Haley because she was on a business lunch.

"Okay, I may or may not have mentioned something like that to Josh, but I hadn't cut my apple into small enough pieces and I was talking to him at the same time. You know I have to chew my food slowly and in small portions."

"Couldn't you have at least waited until after a few more meetings before you mentioned the word *gag* to Joshua DeLong?"

Becca had to admit that she'd come across pretty pathetic on the Skype call with Josh. However, he'd seemed amused and his laughter had been contagious. *I'm still not even sure why he called me.* True, he'd claimed that she'd just been on his mind and he had to call her, but come on. This was Joshua DeLong— the ultimate playboy. Why would he be thinking about Becca at all?

After their meeting on his yacht, she'd researched him a bit more, and in several photos he was pictured beside actresses, models, or women with high cheekbones and perfect figures who had probably never sucked in their stomach a day in their lives. Becca was hardly his type, which was why she had a hard time believing his admission.

"Becca," Stacy said, knocking on the door. "There's someone here to see you."

The fact that Stacy had actually knocked was enough to shake Becca from her thoughts.

"Who is it?"

"Joshua DeLong." *Of course it's him.* That explained why Stacy was on her best behavior. "He wants to take you to lunch."

Leanna squealed. "This is perfect! You can redeem yourself from your last conversation."

"I'm not going to lunch with him. I have too much to do." *And I've embarrassed myself enough for one week.*

"You have to go," Leanna said as she coaxed Becca out of her chair. "He probably finalized the paperwork and just wants to go over it with you."

"She's right," Stacy said. "He mentioned some kind of paperwork, too."

Just great. She'd only known Josh for a week and already he was disrupting her predictable lifestyle.

"But look at what I'm wearing." Becca glanced down at her black slacks and simple black blazer that covered her beige blouse. Her outfit was hardly suitable for having lunch with a man like Joshua DeLong.

"You're a beautiful woman," Leanna said. "Here, let's just make a few changes." Leanna pulled off her jacket and unbuttoned the first three buttons of her blouse.

"That's too many," Becca said as she buttoned up two of the three.

Leanna frowned. "Can we compromise at unbuttoning at least two?"

Becca nodded her head. "I can work with two."

"Well, I definitely want you to 'work it,' but how about we just focus on getting you through the lunch for now. Here, let's change shoes. I think we wear the same size." Leanna kicked off her black heels.

Becca glanced down at her beige ballerina shoes. "What's wrong with my shoes?"

Leanna blinked rapidly. "Sweetie, you can't dine with a man like Joshua DeLong wearing flats."

Becca shrugged. "I suppose you have a point." She easily slipped her feet into the heels. She wasn't a stranger to high-heeled shoes, and putting on Leanna's reminded her how much she'd missed them.

Leanna stepped back and admired the wardrobe changes. "Perfect. Now all you have to do is take your hair out of that tight bun."

Becca swatted Leanna's hands away. "No way I'm taking down my bun. My hair will not cooperate in this Miami summer heat right now without my products."

"Hello? I own my own hair and beauty salon." Leanna lifted the bag on her shoulder. "I always bring hair reinforcements with me."

"Sorry, hon, but your magic bag of tricks is going to have to make an appearance at another time. I refuse to change my hair for a business lunch."

Leanna and Stacy shared a look. "Okay, I guess this is good for now," Leanna said. "Now go out there and redeem yourself from the last conversation." Leanna slapped her butt for good measure, causing Becca to laugh. Unfortunately, her laughter was short-lived, because she turned the corner and focused her gaze on Josh, who was standing near the reception desk.

You can do this, she thought as she approached. Unlike their first meeting, he was dressed in business casual clothing—maroon slacks with a light blue button-up and his Ray-Bans. His blue suede shoes complemented the entire outfit. When Josh saw her, he removed his

Ray-Bans and once again, she was temporarily entranced in his beautiful baby blues.

"Hello, Becca," he said as she approached. "It's nice to see you again."

"Hello, Josh." *Try not to stare so hard at his pearly whites.* "What brings you by our office?"

"I was hoping that we could have lunch and go over the final paperwork." He briefly glanced over her shoulder at something behind her. Becca figured it was Leanna and Stacy, who were ready to jump in if she declined his lunch offer.

"Sure, I'm available for lunch."

"Great, I'm parked right outside. If it's okay with you, I'll drive us to the restaurant and drop you back off after."

"That's fine." She briefly waved at Leanna and Stacy as she followed Josh outside. The minute she stepped out onto the sidewalk, she froze.

"Oh my God," she said, walking toward the gorgeous vehicle parked in front of her office. "Does this breathtaking beauty belong to you?"

"Um, yes," Josh said with a laugh. "This is one of my vehicles."

One of? Becca had a few guilty pleasures, and luxury cars had to be in her top five. "May I?" she asked, itching to run her fingers across the smooth steel.

"Sure." Josh didn't look phased by her request, which only increased her boldness. She felt like her hand moved in slow motion as she touched the exterior of the car.

"I take it you like luxury vehicles?" Josh asked. "It's a—"

"French blue Bugatti Chiron. It goes as fast as two

hundred and sixty miles per hour and is one of the most powerful luxury vehicles in the world." Becca hadn't meant to cut him off, but she was salivating over the car. She walked around the entire Bugatti and admired the detail.

"I wish the vehicle was see-through," Becca said, more to herself than Josh. "If it was, I imagine I'd see a sixteen-cylinder engine with double-powered turbochargers and a frame so sexy it would make me want to cry happy tears and thank the inventors for creating such a beautiful piece of art."

After a few more minutes admiring the vehicle, Becca finally looked at Josh. He was standing on the sidewalk with his arms crossed over his chest and a smirk on his face.

"Sorry," she said. "I guess you can say I have a bit of a car fetish."

"There's no need to apologize." He walked over and opened the door for her. "If I was the type of man to get jealous, I'd have stopped you from admiring my car minutes ago. Instead, you just made me more curious about how you developed your love of cars."

Becca smiled as she got into the car, and Josh followed. Neither of them spoke for the first couple minutes of the drive.

"So are you going to make me beg?"

Becca turned to Josh. "Make you beg for what?"

"Are you going to tell me how you know so much about cars, or are you going to make me beg for the details?"

Becca's laughter echoed throughout the car. "Something tells me that a man like you has never had to beg for anything a day in his life."

As the car stopped at a light, Josh met her eyes. "Something tells me that you're the type of woman who would make me beg." His look was intense and one that she hadn't yet seen. "And something tells me that I wouldn't mind begging."

Is he flirting with me? There's no way Joshua De-Long is flirting with me. Yet the minute his lips curled into a side smile, she disregarded her previous thought. For whatever reason, he was flirting with her, and for an even more insane reason, she was liking it.

"Is French okay with you?" Josh asked as they were taken to one of the best seats in the upscale restaurant. Even in the daytime, the dim lighting in the restaurant provided an intimate ambiance.

"French is fine, but I wasn't aware that this was going to be such an extravagant lunch."

Josh glanced around. "This restaurant has the best French food in Miami. The head chef just won another prestigious award."

"I've heard great things about this place," Becca said as she opened her menu.

"I meant to tell you," Josh said, opening his menu, as well. "You look really nice today."

"Thank you," she said with a smile. He noticed that her black-rimmed glasses seemed smaller than the ones he'd seen her wear in her online picture. He actually liked these glasses a lot. They fit her.

He couldn't quite place what was different about her today, but she looked less restricted than he'd seen her look before. He'd meant to comment on it when they were leaving her office, but her enthusiasm over his car had caused him to forget.

If he hadn't needed to discuss the paperwork, he would have been content with watching her admire his Bugatti all day. The excitement he'd seen on her face was enough to keep him entertained for hours. He still wanted to see just how deep her knowledge of cars went, but she'd grown quiet in the car after he'd asked her, so he would wait to bring it up again.

After they placed their order, he took out the paperwork. "Here's the agreement with your suggestions incorporated in the document."

Becca accepted the packet of information and began scrolling through the pages. "Everything looks good." She took out the single sheet of paper. "What's this?"

Josh took out the same sheet from the paperwork sitting in front of him. "Since you and I weren't seeing eye to eye on the gala being widely publicized, I composed a list of celebrities that are not only heavily involved in charity work, but that truly believe in the mission of the organizations they support."

Josh waited patiently as Becca read through the details. She lifted her head from the sheet when she was finished. "This is pretty impressive."

"I'm glad you think so." Josh hadn't known how much he wanted her approval until he'd received it. "I was also thinking that—with your approval—we could reach out to a couple friends I have in the media to get some good publicity for The Aunt Penny Foundation before the gala. When I researched the foundation, it looked like you haven't had any media coverage in at least a year. It would be great practice and help spread the word about all the good you and Haley do."

Josh wasn't sure if Becca really grasped how much he wanted to help The Aunt Penny Foundation in any way he could, but he hoped she had a better idea today than she had before.

"So what do you think?" he asked since he couldn't read her expression. *This woman probably excels at poker.*

"I must say that after our first meeting, I wasn't quite sure that you even knew the definition of 'treading lightly' when it came to the media. But after reading everything you've presented in this paperwork, I'm confident that your ideas are what's best for the foundation right now."

Josh did a mental fist pump. "I'm happy to hear that. I only see brightness in the future of The Aunt Penny Foundation."

They put the paperwork aside just as their food arrived. As usual, lunch was fantastic, and judging by the appreciative sounds coming from Becca, she was enjoying the food just as much as he was.

"Are you really going to make me beg?" Josh asked between bites.

"Are we back on my car fetish?"

"Can you blame me for asking again? It's not every day that someone knows almost as much about my car as I do."

"That's because the Bugatti Chiron is not just any car." Becca took a sip of water. "Any luxury vehicle enthusiast should be able to name one in the top ten just based off a five-second glance."

"Only five seconds? What about a solid twenty?"

"Nope," Becca said, shaking her head. "Would your mother have to stare at you for twenty seconds before identifying you as her child?"

Josh contemplated his answer. "My mother wouldn't

need twenty seconds, but some circumstances may be different."

"People who love luxury vehicles love them as if they were their children. They shouldn't need twenty seconds to identify their child."

Josh took another bite of his food before continuing. "It's not always black-and-white. For example, what if a child was kidnapped at birth, but reunited with their family as a teenager? The parents would need more than twenty seconds to identify that child."

Becca shook her head. "Come on, you know very well what I mean."

"Another example," Josh said snapping his fingers. "A child given up for adoption and reunited with their birth parents after twenty years."

"Not a good one," Becca said. "One of my close friends was given up for adoption and when she reunited with her birth mother at twenty-five, her mother knew who she was immediately."

"So based off what you're saying, if it would have taken you twenty seconds to identify a luxury car, you could have had your title of luxury vehicle enthusiast revoked?"

Becca leaned forward. "It never takes me twenty seconds to identify a luxury car. Ten seconds tops, and even then it's probably because the car was passing by too fast for me to get a good look."

Josh smiled at her confidence. He'd always been a fan of a good debate and it was refreshing to meet a woman who could keep up with him. He glanced out the window of the restaurant at the parking lot. There were numerous vehicles in the lot that he could ask Becca to identify to test her theory. The prestigious restaurant was crawling with money, and with money came expensive cars.

"If you're going to ask me to identify one of the luxury cars in the parking lot, don't bother," Becca said as she took a sip of water.

"Why not, Ms. Wright? Afraid you'll misidentify a vehicle and prove your theory false?"

Becca leaned back in her chair. "Quite the contrary, Mr. DeLong. The reason I told you not to bother is because I already identified all the luxury cars in the parking lot in the thirty seconds it took for us to exit your vehicle and enter the restaurant."

Josh shook his head. "Yeah, right. I'll believe it when I hear it."

The smirk that crossed Becca's lips gave him fair warning that he should prepare to be wowed. "I'll skip your French blue baby and start with mentioning the Mercedes-Benz S-Class in the far right corner of the lot. Then there's a Mercedes-Benz E-Class two cars down from it. Two BMW 4 Series—one gray and the other white. A brilliant yellow Lamborghini Aventador parked next to the white BMW. A Lexus ES parked in the left corner two spaces away from a classic 1966 Jaguar. And although I'm sure, just like you, most of the owners of the vehicles used valet parking, the smartest owner is the one who probably paid the valet extra to park his or her sexy red 1958 Ferrari 250 GT LWB California Spider in the only semi-discreet spot in the parking lot. That spot also happens to be the closest to the valet desk. You don't leave classics like the Ferrari unattended for long. The Jaguar owner should probably take notes from the Ferrari owner."

Josh tried his best to keep a straight face. *Who in*

the world is this woman? He was rarely speechless, but Becca had completely stolen the words from his mouth. There was something about her that challenged him, and finding a woman who truly challenged him had been so difficult, he'd often thought that such a woman didn't exist. At least, she hadn't existed until Becca Wright.

"In case you haven't done the math, it should have taken me forty-five seconds to name all nine luxury cars in the lot, but you and I both know it didn't take that long to walk into the restaurant." Becca took another sip of her water. "And there's no need to tell me that you're impressed because I can read it in your eyes."

Her satisfied smile was wide and it caused him to smile right back. Everything she'd said was right. He was impressed. More than he had been in a very long time.

Chapter 5

"Earth to Josh? Are you going to stare at that basketball all day, or are we actually going to hoop with it?"

Josh turned to face his youngest brother, Logan. "The others aren't even here yet."

"Exactly. Which means we can practice until they get here."

Josh threw Logan the ball. At least twice a month, Josh met up with his three younger brothers for a two-on-two basketball game in the outdoor court down the street from their childhood home, before they all headed to their mother's house for Sunday dinner. As usual, his brothers Ryan and Sebastian were late.

"Is everything going okay with work?" Logan asked. "You've seemed distracted since you got here."

"Work's been crazy." Josh rebounded for Logan as he shot from the free throw line. "Do you remember that tech company I was telling you about?"

"The one that you just had to do a massive layoff for?"

"Yes, that's the one." Josh and Logan switched places so that Josh was the one shooting. "Most of the employees loved the management team, so letting go some of the key players wasn't easy. I've been in numerous meetings with the remaining management staff trying to defuse the situation. The culture of this company is great and I really don't want to change it. Unfortunately, the staff don't understand my decisions yet and until they do, there are a lot of growing pains ahead."

"Don't sweat it, big bro. You've had to make some difficult decisions throughout your career, but you're doing what's best for the company."

"I wish they saw it that way, because right now I feel like I'm demolishing dreams and breaking what was otherwise a close camaraderie between colleagues." And turning friends against each other. Just this morning he'd had one of the executives call him to rat out one of his friends and fellow executives who he believed had been secretly stealing money from the company years ago. Josh had his team investigating the situation, and he had a feeling the outcome wasn't going to be pretty.

"Hey," Logan said, getting his attention. "Do you remember when I was ten and you were fifteen and you walked me to my friend's house because he was moving after his dad lost his job?"

"Yeah, I remember."

"When we arrived at their house, we walked right into an argument. My friend's dad was trying to explain to his wife that some investors had just begun cleaning house and laying people off without even meeting with the staff first."

"That's right." Josh went for another shot and missed. "He also mentioned that the main investor was a corporate raider who didn't give a damn about anyone or anything as long as he was making money."

"And after that conversation you said there was no way you'd ever become a corporate raider and change the course of someone's life without giving your decisions a second thought."

Josh stopped shooting the ball. "And lo and behold, I became the exact person I claimed I would never become."

"No, you didn't," Logan said. "Bro, despite what some of those articles may say, you actually care about what happens to the companies you invest in. True, you've had to be somewhat ruthless to get where you are today, but that's just the nature of the business. For years, you've managed to maintain your dignity while also keeping your emotions out of the situation. Don't start doubting yourself now that you're at the top of your game."

Josh let Logan's words sink in. His brother had basically summarized all the fears he had in that one statement. "You're right. I need to get out of my headspace."

"Better yet," Logan said, "maybe you should find a sweet honey to help you get out of your headspace." Josh's thoughts immediately went to Becca, as they had a lot lately.

"Are you sure you're not the older brother?" Josh asked, finally landing a shot without even hitting the backboard.

Logan pretended to smooth out his hair and T-shirt. "I've been trying to tell you for years that I'm the most fly DeLong man in the family, but y'all don't want to listen."

"That's because you're too full of yourself," Ryan said as he walked onto the court with Sebastian. "Men who really have swag don't need to vocalize the fact that they have swag. They just exude it." All four brothers dabbed fists and prepared to start the game.

"I just have to make a quick call." Josh walked over to his gym bag that he'd placed on the steel bleachers and pulled out his phone to call Becca. She answered on the third ring.

"Hey, Josh."

For a second, Josh soaked in her warm voice. "Hey, Becca. How are you?"

"I'm fine. Just busy as usual. How are you?"

"I'm good, but I'd be even better if you'd accompany me to an exclusive black-tie movie premiere at a waterfront estate in the North Bay Road neighborhood on Tuesday."

"A movie premiere? So it wouldn't be for business?"

"It would be great for networking and spreading the word about The Aunt Penny Foundation," Josh said, although he hadn't been thinking about business when he'd decided to invite her. He'd simply wanted to spend some more time with her. He really liked her. However, he wasn't sure if it was just the challenge that amused him, or if it was more. He needed to find out and the more time they spent together, the quicker he'd figure it out.

"Also, the host of the movie premiere is a business associate, so I have to make an appearance. I'd be honored if you'd attend with me because I really don't want to go stag."

Since he couldn't see her in person, he couldn't gauge if she was leaning more toward saying yes or no. His brothers motioned for him to join the game and he waved them off.

"Okay, I'll go with you," she finally said.

"Great," Josh said with a big smile. "I'll email you the details. Would 6:00 p.m. work?"

"Yes, that's fine."

Josh disconnected the call and joined his brothers on the court. Now that Becca had agreed to accompany him to the movie premiere, his week was already looking better.

Becca tried her best not to elbow the strangers who were rudely pushing past her in the crowded sandwich café as she and Haley made their way to the table where Leanna was already seated.

"Jeez," she huffed when they sat down. "Why is it so packed today?"

Leanna laughed. "Well, besides the fact that it's lunchtime on a Tuesday, they're also handing out free red-and-blue sandwiches in honor of Independence Day this week."

"Ew," Haley said. "That sounds disgusting. I'm afraid to even ask what's in it."

Leanna took a sip of green tea. "You'll see for yourselves when they bring ours to the table. When I ordered our usual, they asked if we wanted to try the sandwiches and I agreed."

"If you two don't like them I can bring them to Stacy."

"So you went from being ready to fire her to bringing her sandwiches?" Leanna asked. "I must be working at my salon too much, because last time I was in the office, Stacy wasn't doing much work."

Becca shrugged. "She's growing on me. When I called the temp agency, they mentioned this job would be her last strike, and by the end of their apology I was telling them we would keep her on."

Becca still needed to have a serious talk with the teenager about her work ethic, but she was hoping after that conversation Stacy would work harder.

"Okay, so enough about that." Haley clasped her hands in front of her. "Are you going to tell us more about this event that Josh invited you to tonight?"

Becca knew the minute Haley asked if she wanted to meet Leanna for lunch that they would ask for details about her conversation with Josh. "Since I had a feeling you both would ask me a ton of questions, I printed out the event invitation he emailed me."

Leanna and Haley both reviewed the sheet of paper. "Oh my God," Leanna said. "You're going to that exclusive movie premiere that everyone is talking about? It doesn't even release for another few months."

Becca nodded her head. "Yeah, and I love action movies, so it will definitely be a treat."

"And it's a black-tie movie premiere in the North Bay Road neighborhood?" Haley exclaimed. "I know I don't need to remind you that only the rich and famous stay there. I can't believe you're going to such a high-profile event and you seem so unfazed."

Oh, she wasn't unfazed. As a matter of fact, she was nervous about tonight and had contemplated canceling before she thought about how great it would be to spread the word about the foundation to a group of affluent people.

"I'm so excited for you," Leanna squealed. "What are you going to wear?"

"I'm thinking about wearing the dress I wore for the awards banquet we had last year for our graduating students."

Haley touched Becca's arm. "You can't be serious. An occasion like this calls for an exquisite dress." The moment Haley looked at Leanna, Becca knew she wasn't going to like what came next.

"I think today we're closing the office early," Haley said with a sneaky smile. "We're long overdue for a girls' shopping trip and Leanna and I need to help you get ready for tonight."

"I don't want to fuss over my clothes and makeup," Becca said, shaking her head. "This isn't a date, so how I look shouldn't matter."

Haley gave her a look of disbelief. "Oh, come on, Becca, I know you too well to think you actually believe that. Are you really trying to convince us that you don't find him attractive?"

"Of course he's gorgeous and downright sexy. I know it. He knows it. And so does the majority of the population in Miami. But I would no sooner sleep with him than fly to the moon."

Haley lifted an eyebrow. "No one said anything about sleeping with him, but the fact that you mentioned it means that you've at least thought about it."

Yes, I've thought about it! What woman wouldn't think about sex when staring into the blue eyes of Joshua DeLong? "Even if I have, that's beside the point."

"Oh no, sweetie," Leanna said. "I think that's exactly the point."

"Have you seen the type of beautiful women he dates?" Becca asked. "Each one is more beautiful than the last, so I can't see what he'd want with a woman of substance like me."

"Becca, you are just as beautiful as all those women, if not more. You just choose not to flaunt your wonderful assets."

Becca eyed Haley skeptically. "You sound like my mother."

Haley shook her head. "I'm just telling the truth. You're a total knockout when you put in the effort and I think Joshua DeLong would fall to his knees if he saw you dressed up."

Becca glanced down at her plain white blouse and typical black slacks. The outfit wasn't much to look at. There was a time she'd really put effort into the way she looked, but somewhere along the way she'd lost sight of focusing on herself. Regardless, she wasn't sure she could go through with a mini makeover before tonight.

When their food came, neither woman pushed Becca any further and instead began talking about something else. As they neared the end of their meal, Becca addressed the situation again.

"I think the dress I wore to the banquet will be fine. There's no need to get dolled up." Becca could feel Haley observing her as she took the last bite of her chicken Caesar salad.

"What are you afraid of?" Haley asked. "That Josh won't find you attractive?"

"That's not it." Becca looked up from her plate. "I guess a part of me is afraid that he would." *And if he does, how will I handle his advances?* The last thing Becca wanted was to develop feelings for a man like Josh—the type of man who discarded women without a second thought. If he already flirted with her as regular plain-Jane Becca, how would she handle his advances when he flirted with Becca 2.0? She'd been there and done that with men like him, and she wasn't trying to repeat past experiences.

Judging by the sly smile on Haley's face, she'd known Becca's fear all along and just wanted to hear her admit it. Haley glanced at Leanna before pulling Becca from her seat. "No more excuses. When Joshua picks you up tonight, he won't know what hit him."

Haley shook her head. "Nope, I don't like that one, either."

Becca frowned as she went back to the fitting room to try on the last dress they'd picked out. Leanna was waiting for them at her salon to finalize Becca's quickie makeover. Already, Becca and Haley had been to several stores and being the shopaholic that she was, Haley had already convinced her to purchase several new outfits for everyday wear and three dresses so that she could get rid of any dress she'd formerly worn to a banquet.

After she pulled the strapless dress over her breasts, Becca glanced in the mirror. "Oh my goodness," she said to herself. "It's beautiful." The elegant dress was midnight blue and form-fitted, stopping right above her knees. A sash on the side of the dress added an extra amount of flair to the piece. Becca had been trying on all the dresses with a pair of four-inch glittery silver heels that she assumed would be too flashy, yet with this dress, the entire outfit was…perfect.

Haley gasped when Becca stepped out of the fitting room. "That's it! That's the winner."

"I agree." Becca looked at herself in the floor-length mirror outside the fitting room. It had been a long time since she had seen herself look so beautiful. Becca rarely talked about her family because over the past five years, her relationship with her parents and older sister had become even more strained. She was tired of being considered a disappointment to them, and somewhere along the way of trying to prove to them that she was her own woman, she'd lost sight of herself. As she looked at Haley in the mirror, the moment almost brought tears to her eyes.

Haley walked over and hugged her. "Welcome back, bestie. You've been gone for a while."

Becca laughed. "Thanks for being patient with me." They stood there for a few more seconds before Becca went to change. After purchasing the dress, they made their way to Leanna's salon. Leanna was already waiting for them when they entered.

Becca was seated in Leanna's salon chair before she could even catch her breath.

"Becca, Becca, Becca," Leanna said, immediately taking down her tight bun. "I've waited so long to get my hands into this thick velvety hair."

Becca loved her hair, but her life was so busy that she often didn't have time to style it. She'd always chosen to wear her hair naturally curly even before the natural look was the new "it" thing. Her thick and curly dark brown locks cascaded down her back. She assumed if she straightened her hair, it would almost be to her waist.

"But before I dive into your hair, I want you to go to one of the back rooms with Sherry."

"Who's Sherry?"

"I'm Sherry."

Becca turned to face the perky woman with the tiny voice who'd spoken. Becca stood as Leanna introduced them. Sherry towered over Becca's five-foot-six-inch frame by six to eight inches, which was why the tiny voice surprised Becca.

Unlike Leanna's pink highlights, Sherry had bright blue highlights. Becca didn't know what she did in the salon, but she liked her positive attitude.

Becca was so busy observing Sherry's black-and-red top that she hadn't heard Leanna explain why she had to see Sherry.

"What do I have to do?"

"Time to level the playing field," Leanna said as she grabbed her shoulders and motioned for her to follow Sherry, who'd already started walking to the back.

"Time to do what?"

Leanna looked to Haley. Haley cleared her throat. "It's time to smooth out that diamond."

Smooth out that diamond? What is she talking about? A couple of the other women in the salon began snickering, so Becca assumed they'd already caught on to whatever Leanna and Haley were saying. "Still not following."

Sherry stopped walking and turned around with a smile. "Your friends are trying to find an easy way of saying that it's time for me to wax your lady parts. I assume it's because they don't want to make you nervous."

Becca's mouth dropped open. "Absolutely not. There's no way that's happening."

"Oh yes. It's happening," Haley said, pushing her toward the room. "Sherry's great, so you're in good hands. She specializes in the chocolate wax, so it doesn't hurt."

"Did you just say chocolate? As in, she is going to wax my lady parts with chocolate? Like the chocolate you eat?"

"Well, obviously you won't be eating the chocolate, silly," Sherry said. "Although we have had a few female clients ask if they can buy a jar and take it home to use on their partners. I'm personally more into licking chocolate off my man rather than waxing him with it, but hey, I don't judge."

Chocolate waxing? Becca felt nauseous.

Haley pulled her to the side. "In college, didn't you always tell me that it was better to be overprepared than underprepared? Just look at this as a way of watering your flower garden so that those seeds you planted can bloom. Your garden can't water itself and the last thing you want is for your nosy neighbor who loves gardening to look at your flower bed and see dead roses."

"Okay, I get it," Becca said shaking her head. "Enough with the metaphors." She cracked her neck and rolled her shoulders. "I can do this. It's no big deal."

"Right," Haley said with a smile. "It's no big deal."

Five minutes later, Becca was lying on the waxing table regretting her decision as she waited for Sherry to enter. When Sherry knocked on the door, Becca felt relieved. The sooner Sherry started waxing her with chocolate, the sooner she could get it over with.

Becca leaned back when Sherry sat down on her

stool. "Hello!" Sherry said in her perky voice. Becca's head flew up.

"Did you just say *hello* to my private area?" *That can't be normal.*

"Once you've seen one, you've seen them all," Sherry said. "But, dear, I have to ask. How long has it been since you waxed?"

"I've never waxed. I've only trimmed."

Sherry gave her a blank stare. "So Haley was right. You are a wax virgin."

Goodness, she makes it sound so dirty. "Yes, you could say that. Is that okay?"

"Yes, it's fine." Sherry got out a few more tools. "I'm just going to do a little trimming before your wax. Is that okay?"

"Um, yeah, that's fine. I guess it's been a while since I've trimmed."

Sherry started trimming. "Do you know why most women prefer chocolate wax?"

"No, I don't. I hadn't heard of it before today."

"That's not surprising. Chocolate wax is a growing trend and has many benefits. For example, there are many anti-inflammatory properties in chocolate, so overall, it's more soothing and less painful."

"That's interesting." Becca tried to relax and ignore the fact that this was the most action her private area had seen in years.

"It sure is. Okay, now I'm going to start waxing." Becca heard some clicking and clacking, indicating that Sherry was preparing the wax.

"Another reason so many women prefer chocolate is because it releases endorphins and improves your overall mood."

"So it has the same benefits as when you eat chocol— Ahh!" Becca's head flew up again when Sherry pulled the first strip of wax. "I thought this was supposed to be less painful."

"It is, dear," Sherry said as she pulled another strip. "In your case, there's a lot going on down here, so this first time may be a little painful. But after I finish with you today, your body will feel so much better and you'll be dying to come back."

"What do you mean 'my body'?" Becca asked after a squeal.

"Oh, Leanna and Haley didn't tell you?"

"Tell me what?" Becca said through gritted teeth.

"They told me to give you a full body wax, and in my experience wax virgins get too nervous about me waxing their private area if I start with their legs or underarms. So I changed the order."

Becca would have argued about the situation, but it was no use.

The rest of the makeover went a lot smoother than the waxing, including the triple-deep conditioner treatment Leanna had given her curls.

A few hours later, she stood in front of her bedroom mirror, ready to show her friends her final look before Josh arrived in twenty minutes to pick her up. She had to admit that she didn't only look beautiful, but felt beautiful, as well.

"Okay, guys, here I come." She turned the corner to her kitchen and did a spin for her friends. When she stopped to look at them, she caught them high-fiving each other.

"You look amazing," Leanna said. "Definitely ready for a night with the rich and famous."

When Becca looked at Haley, she had tears in her eyes. "You look gorgeous, Becca. You're going to blow his mind."

Becca dabbed at the corner of her own eyes as she smiled at Haley. "Thanks for bringing me back, Haley."

"Anytime, bestie. Anytime."

Chapter 6

Josh stepped out of the vehicle he'd reserved for the evening, and adjusted his navy blue suit jacket. He was glad that he hadn't chosen the typical stretch limousine. For a car enthusiast like Becca, an everyday limo wouldn't do.

He walked toward the complex she lived in. She'd given him instructions to call when he was five minutes away, so that's precisely what he'd done. He'd briefly wondered if she hadn't wanted him to see her place, but hadn't pressed her on the issue.

On the way over, he'd picked up a single pink rose to give to her. Josh had always wanted to give a single rose to a woman, but in the past the women he'd dated had expected a full bouquet, and some had gone so far as to interpret the different rose colors. If he got the wrong color, the consequences weren't always pretty.

Remember, man, this isn't a date. He'd been reminding himself of that since he'd asked her to accompany him. Yet no matter how many times he chanted those words, it still felt like he was about to go on a date. He hadn't felt this enthusiastic about seeing a woman in a really long time, so he welcomed the feeling.

Josh walked into the building and was headed toward the security desk when he heard someone call his name. He scanned the handful of people in the lobby area and stopped when his eyes landed on a pair of silky brown legs getting up from one of the chairs.

"Damn," he said, louder than expected. Usually he was better at masking his initial reaction, but the breathtaking beauty in midnight blue walking his way was making him forget all the tricks he usually used.

It still looked like Becca, but gone were the bland oversize clothes, black-rimmed glasses and tight bun. They'd been replaced with an elegant, form-fitted dress and sexy heels. She wasn't wearing her glasses, so he assumed she was wearing contacts. He noticed everything about her as she walked toward him, but what had his mouth hung wide open was her striking hairstyle.

When her hair was in a bun, he couldn't tell she had beautiful dark brown elongated curls. Tonight, it was pulled to one side and cascaded around her shoulders and back. He itched to run his fingers through it to see if it was as soft as it looked. When she stood in front of him, he noticed that she was wearing the perfect amount of makeup. Not too much and not too little. And her lips looked downright kissable in her red lipstick. He'd always had a thing for red lipstick, which made not pulling her in for a kiss extremely difficult.

"Hello, Josh."

"Hi, Becca," he managed. "You look absolutely beautiful."

"Thanks," she said with a smile. "You do, too. And I really like your haircut." Earlier in the day, Josh had decided to change up his hairstyle and get the sides of his hair cut into a fade, leaving only the top curly and trimmed.

She glanced at his hand. "Is that for me?"

Josh looked at the rose. "Sorry, yes, this is for you." He handed her the pink rose. "I saw it and thought about you."

She brought the rose to her nose and inhaled, keeping her eyes on him the entire time. "Thank you. I love it."

Her voice was so soft when she spoke. *I wonder if her bedroom voice is just as soft...* He blinked to erase the image of her in his bed. *This is not a date. This is not a date.*

"Are you ready to go?"

"Sure."

She walked out the door first, giving him a great view of her round backside. He followed her and looked to the sky when they stepped outside. *She's trying to kill me.* There was no way he could focus on a movie premiere with her looking as good as she did.

He loosened the collar on his dress shirt and almost ran into her when she stopped in her tracks and squealed. "You're kidding me! It's been years since I've seen a white 1986 eight-seater Lincoln Excalibur with gold trimmings."

Josh laughed. "Damn, you're good. I figured you'd appreciate something more than a regular limo."

"You thought right," Becca said, walking around the vehicle. After she was finished checking out the details, the driver opened the limo door for them to enter. Becca performed a thorough examination of the interior, just as she had with the exterior of the car. Josh was content to just sit back and watch her.

"I'm beginning to notice a pattern."

She glanced his way. "And what might that be?"

He observed her legs as she sat back in her seat next to him. They looked silky and smooth and once again he had to reel back his desire to touch her. "I notice that you aren't satisfied until you're sure you've covered every detail of the car and haven't missed anything. It's almost as if your mind goes through a checklist of everything you know about the car and you need to make sure everything is as it should be."

Becca smiled. "You're right, that's exactly what I usually do. Oftentimes, I have a checklist in my mind that I'm working my way through. Not just with cars, but with everything."

"Must be exhausting. To live life based off a checklist rather than living in the moment."

"Oh, come on," she said with a laugh. "I doubt you got to where you are today without setting goals for yourself."

"You're right, I set goals for myself. But I guess I prefer to set big ones. I'm not really a meticulous goal-setting type of guy." When she hitched an eyebrow, he laughed. "For the record, I'm not judging you. I'm merely inquiring if your checklists allow for much spontaneity."

Her face softened. She briefly glanced out the window as they turned into the North Bay Road neighborhood, then offered Josh a nice view of her profile.

"I guess my life doesn't allow for much spontaneity,

but as of recently, I've decided to make a few changes." She turned to face him. "Starting with accepting your offer to accompany you tonight. A couple weeks ago, I would have declined in an instant. But now… Now, I was too curious to pass it up."

It wasn't so much what she said but how she said it that got his attention. Up until now, he'd done most of the flirting, and even then it had been minimal compared to how much he actually wanted to flirt with her. However, when she talked the way she just did, he wasn't sure how much longer he could convince himself to keep things friendly.

Does she have any idea the effect she has on me?

"We're here," the driver said, stopping the car and then opening the door for them. Although he knew they needed to exit the vehicle, Josh was much more interested in continuing to hold Becca's stare. After a few more silent seconds, he exited the car and offered his hand to her. When his hand closed over hers, he felt a jolt course through his body that he hadn't felt in a long time.

He was so wrapped up in Becca that he didn't notice they were on the red carpet until a light flashed. When the photographer asked them to pose, he took his cue from Becca and was surprised when she posed. They took a few more photos and made their way to the lavish gardens of the grand estate where the pre-premiere event was taking place.

"Are you okay?" he whispered.

She glanced at him. "Are you asking me that because they took several pictures of us together?"

"Yes. I know how much you dislike the paparazzi."

She gave him a side smile and lightly tapped him on

the chest. "Come on. Let's go mingle and spread the word about The Aunt Penny Foundation." She grabbed a glass of wine from one of the servers and began making her way through the crowd.

The place was swarming with the rich and famous, yet Becca wasn't fazed by those present. Instead of getting lost in the crowd, she was working her charm and socializing with ease. Josh realized two things in that moment. One, Becca was a rare find—intelligent, beautiful, with just the right amount of sass. And two, after preaching to his brothers about the fact that he could read a woman a mile away, he finally had to swallow his words. Becca Wright had layers and just when he thought he had her figured out, she surprised him.

Becca had to admit the night was going better than she'd anticipated. The pre-event had gone fantastically and she'd been able to raise a lot of interest in The Aunt Penny Foundation. The actual movie premiere had gone great, as well, and Becca had no doubt that when the action movie hit the theaters, it would be a hit.

However, the highlight of the night had definitely been Josh's reaction to her. When he'd initially spotted her in the lobby of her complex, she'd been surprised at the blatant attraction she'd seen in his eyes. If he'd been trying to hold back the effect she was having on him, he hadn't done a good job.

During the entire pre-event, she'd caught Josh stealing glances of her when he thought she wasn't paying attention. She'd wanted to tell him that there was no way she could miss the looks he was shooting her way. Even if she didn't physically catch him, her body could feel when his eyes were on her. She felt alive. Desired.

Now they were back at the estate for the after-party, on a part of the grounds that had previously been closed off. Long sheer curtains hung from two rows of pillars and plush modern furniture was strategically placed across the grounds. Liquor and food stations were set up throughout it all. But her favorite part of the decor was the glass dance floor that had been placed over the exquisite pool.

The only thing that would make the night even better was if she hadn't been stuck talking to a man she'd never cared for.

"Ms. Wright, I must say I'm impressed by what you and Haley Adams are doing at The Aunt Penny Foundation." *A compliment from Judge Chapmen? The world must be ending.*

"Thank you, Judge Chapmen. We're very proud of the foundation."

"Well, you have to be, don't you?" Judge Chapmen said with a boastful laugh. "You're not putting your Ivy League education to good use, so if it fails, you basically have to start from the bottom again."

And there's the insult I was expecting. "Actually, I'm putting my Ivy League education to great use. There are a lot of different career paths one can take—"

"Nonprofit work isn't a credible career for a woman such as yourself."

Becca squinted. "And what type of woman is that?"

"A single woman trying to make a living on her own. The work you do could be done by anyone. You don't even need a college degree, let alone an Ivy League degree. It's more suitable as a hobby for a stay-at-home wife who is already supported financially by her husband."

Lord, give me strength. Becca started counting backward in her mind, trying to calm her annoyance. "Judge Chapmen, I don't expect someone like you to understand the type of work I do, nor should you expect for me to allow you to disrespect me and my line of work."

"Someone like me? What is that supposed to mean?"

"You know what it means. Small-minded. Unwilling to see women as equals instead of accessories. The type of man who thinks the world revolves around money."

Judge Chapmen took a step closer, irritation evident in his posture. "When you were a young girl, I thought you had a promising future. Your parents sent you to the best schools. They placed you in the best programs. You had the potential to make a great wife to my son, but instead you became a disgrace to society."

"A disgrace to whose society?" she asked, her voice getting a little louder. She ignored those around her who turned their heads. "You may be friends with my parents, but that doesn't give you the right to talk to me any way you please. I never would have married your son and I feel sorry for the woman who finally did marry him."

"How dare you—"

"Is everything okay here?" Josh chose that moment to approach. He looked from Becca to Judge Chapmen.

"Everything is fine," Becca said, never taking her eyes off the judge. "Judge Chapmen was just leaving, weren't you?"

Instead of taking the hint and leaving, Judge Chapmen continued. "I feel sorry for your parents. They had such high hopes for you, but you failed them." With that, he finally left.

Becca wasn't sure how long she stood there looking

at the empty space where Judge Chapmen had been standing. She jumped when Josh touched her arm.

"Are you okay?" he asked with concern. "What was that about?"

Becca sighed. "I'm fine, just a little on edge. Judge Chapmen and my dad are old friends. They went to law school together."

"Oh, okay." She could tell by the inquisitive look in his eyes that he wanted to ask her more. She wondered how much he'd heard. She couldn't recall when Josh had approached, so depending on when he'd walked into the conversation, he could have heard her mention Judge Chapmen's son.

"Are you ready to go?" Josh asked. "I think we've done enough networking for one night."

"Actually, I am ready to leave." Judge Chapmen had put her in a bad mood. "I've lost my ability to put on a fake smile." She'd done that throughout most of her life, and she wasn't going to resurrect bad habits.

"That's fine by me." As Josh said a few goodbyes, she wondered if he noticed the stares she was receiving from a few of the attendees. She had no doubt that the upturned noses were a result of her conversation with Judge Chapmen.

Once they were seated in the vehicle, Becca let out a breath she hadn't known she'd been holding. "I'm sorry if I embarrassed you."

Josh was already shaking his head. "You didn't embarrass me, Becca. You could never embarrass me. And standing up to a man who was trying to degrade you is not something you ever have to apologize for."

She studied his eyes. She knew a lot of men who would have chastised her for speaking the way she had to a judge. "I love my family, but I've never cared too much for the people they associate themselves with." Her mind drifted to her sixteenth birthday. That was the day she truly realized that the goals her parents had set for her weren't the same goals she had for herself. Up until that point, she'd held on to the hope that she'd been wrong.

"You need to get out of your headspace," Josh said, breaking her thoughts. "There's a private park nearby that I have access to. The Moguls own it. Would you like to take a walk in the park? Maybe clear your mind?"

"That's a good idea."

Josh gave the driver directions to the park. "We should be there in no time."

She smiled. "You continue to surprise me, Joshua DeLong."

His laugh filled the car. "If that isn't the pot calling the kettle black."

Chapter 7

"Are you cold?" Josh asked when he noticed Becca shiver.

She gave him a small smile. "Just a little."

Josh took off his suit jacket and placed it over her shoulders. "I hate to cover up that dress, but I guess it's better than having you shiver the entire time we walk." Her laugh was music to his ears. He didn't like seeing her upset.

"I needed that laugh," Becca said. "I try to avoid Judge Chapmen at all costs, but Miami isn't that big."

"You mentioned that he went to school with your father. Is your father a judge or a lawyer?"

"My father's a judge as well, but Judge Chapmen likes to be in the spotlight all the time, so I'm not surprised he was in attendance tonight."

Josh led them to his favorite path with palm trees

lining either side. They began walking in comfortable silence as the trees lightly swayed in the wind.

"Have you ever convinced yourself that you were over a particular situation and could handle the repercussions of a decision you made, only to realize that maybe you're not as over it as you thought?"

"All the time," Josh said. "Of course, depending on the situation I might try to mask my reaction, but sometimes I feel like my true feelings are written across my face."

They walked in silence a little bit longer before Becca spoke again. "Growing up, I was the walking definition of an overachiever. I taught myself to read at four. I excelled in all my school subjects. I won so many violinist awards that folks joked about me playing with the symphony at the Arsht Center one day."

"That's quite an accomplishment."

"It is. I haven't played in a while. I miss it." Becca sighed. "On top of all that, every time I attended an event that my parents would force me to attend, I played the role of adorable daughter with the potential to become the perfect trophy wife."

"That sounds awful."

"It was awful. Even though I was good at a lot of things, my shortcomings were definitely of the social nature. It didn't take long for my classmates to shun me as a 'Goody Two-shoes.' For years, I ignored them and assumed they were jealous of my academic prowess. Until one day I looked in the mirror and realized they were right—I was a nerd in every sense of the word. But that was okay with me."

Josh observed her. "I'm assuming based on that

faraway look in your eyes, it wasn't okay with your family?"

"My older sister, Allison, played the role better than most. She landed a rich and nice husband—a rare combination in the type of neighborhood I grew up in—and she has three children. She just started her own catering business and after ten years of marriage she's never seemed happier. In my parents' eyes, Allison is everything that they hoped I would be. The perfect wife and mother."

"What about The Aunt Penny Foundation? Were they on board when you initially mentioned the foundation to them?"

"Actually, they were," Becca said with a smile. "I've been attending fundraisers and charities since before I could walk. I was even able to get financial commitment from my family and other connections with deep pockets to help get The Aunt Penny Foundation off the ground. My parents may not feel as though what I do for a living is ideal, but saying that I 'failed them,' as Judge Chapmen so eloquently put it, is a bit harsh."

Josh shook his head. "That man is a piece of work, but at least your parents are supportive."

"*Were* supportive," Becca said in a low voice. "Like I said, Judge Chapmen was harsh with his words, but they weren't entirely untrue. I'm still not married, and in their eyes I'm too old to be without a husband and family of my own."

"Sometimes doing what we love has consequences."

Becca slowed her stride and glanced at him. "Are you speaking from experience?"

"I guess you could say that." Josh grabbed a leaf off a tree branch that was hanging low over the path.

"My mother said I came out of the womb arguing, so everyone believed I was going to be a lawyer. No surprise when I went to law school and became president of the law review."

"Wow, that's amazing," Becca said enthusiastically.

"It was, and I assumed being an attorney was in my future. But once I started to practice, I found the pace way too slow. Cases would take months or even years to resolve and I needed more action than that."

Becca laughed. "So you got bored and instead of fighting for justice, you entered the world of corporate raiding?"

Josh mocked offense. "Do I hear judgment in your voice?"

"Not judgment per se, but rather curiosity."

Josh thought back to the early stages of his career when he was willing to try anything and everything in hopes of making a name for himself. "After leaving law, I entered corporate America ready to make up for the time I'd missed. I started by offering legal consulting for small businesses, and before long I was being recruited by large corporations to work for them. I remember visiting my mom and brothers one day and handing my mom a large check. She cried happily for hours that day."

"I can imagine," Becca said with a smile. "So you were practicing law. Then you offered legal counseling for large corporations. Then what?"

Josh smirked. *She's genuinely interested in hearing my story.* He couldn't recall the last time a woman had wanted to know not only Josh DeLong, self-made millionaire, but also Josh DeLong, the man behind the millions.

"There was a company I was consulting for that was being targeted by a venture capitalist. After trying everything they could, they sought my consul. It was my first real introduction to what a corporate raider did. At the time, I didn't have the heart to tell the company that they were fighting a losing battle. They'd made too many poor decisions that had landed them in their predicament. Nevertheless, I was intrigued by the entire ordeal and began to study corporate raiding to fight fire with fire."

"So in the end, did you help the company?"

"Not exactly. My efforts came up short and my legal counseling was no longer needed. A week later, that same venture capitalist reached out to me. Apparently, despite my failed attempt to assist the company, he saw potential and took me under his wing."

"That's a pretty interesting way to enter the field," Becca said, brushing the curls off her face now that the breeze had picked up. "Working with the very enemy you had previously tried to stop."

Josh stopped walking and looked to her. "I'll admit, what I do isn't the most honest career, but I'm not the enemy. The assets of most of the companies I invest in are undervalued. And those that aren't may have a good three to five successful years left if they continue operating with the same standards, and eventually they need to take drastic measures to increase their share value."

Becca studied his eyes. "I can see how you wouldn't think that you're the enemy, but what about those people who lose their jobs? Or the companies who lose everything once you resell their stock? What about that?"

Josh was used to having to defend his career, but for some reason Becca believing the worst of him was a tough pill to swallow. "No career is perfect and I'm sure you'll agree that no one individual is perfect, either."

When her eyes softened, he felt relieved. "Tell me about your brothers," she said as she started walking again. "How many do you have?"

"Three younger brothers. We always thought my mother had hoped my youngest brother, Logan, would be a girl, but she claims she always wanted sons."

"You mentioned your mother and brothers. What about your father?"

Josh briefly glanced up at the moon. "My father passed while I was in college."

"Oh, Josh, I'm so sorry to hear that," Becca said as she briefly placed her hand on his arm. "That must have been so terrible for your family."

Josh took a deep breath. "There's not a day that goes by that I don't think about my father. According to Will DeLong, progress means nothing without struggle." Josh thought back to the last conversation he'd had with his father. Had he known it would be his last, he would have cherished it even more at the time.

"He was one of the most hardworking men I knew. His motto was 'the road to success may be long and hard, but nothing worth having is easy.'"

"I like that," Becca said. "Even though I never knew your father, you can tell what type of a man he was just by his motto."

"Yeah, I'm still trying to figure out my own motto. Do you have words you live by?"

Becca shrugged. "I'm still trying to figure out mine, too. My parents' motto was always 'do things the Wright way,' as in, W-R-I-G-H-T."

"Clever," Josh said with a laugh.

"They sure think so." Becca smiled. "Honestly, I sort of always liked that motto too, but don't tell them that. I'd never hear the end of it."

"Maybe you should tell them that one day," Josh suggested. "We give our parents a hard time, and based on what you've told me you and your parents share different views. But parents need to hear that something they did when raising you worked and stayed with you. Take it from someone who wishes he could have said more, but didn't."

If Becca disagreed, she didn't say so. Instead, she lightly touched his arm again. It may have only been a small form of comfort, but he welcomed the feeling.

As they approached an open gate leading to a section filled with beautiful Floridian flowers and a small pond, Josh grabbed Becca's hand. She enjoyed the way her hand felt enclosed in his. It was a small gesture that she'd rarely shared with the opposite sex.

"Watch your step," Josh said, leading her through the gate and over the stones. When they reached a railing overlooking Biscayne Bay, he released her hand and leaned over the railing.

"Are you afraid of heights?" he asked.

"Not at all." Becca leaned beside him against the railing.

"So," Josh said as he clasped his hands together, "are you going to tell me how you almost married the judge's son?"

Ah, so he did hear me. "I hadn't known if you'd heard that part of the conversation or not."

"Yeah, I heard it. I debated whether I should mention it to you, but my curiosity is getting the best of me."

Becca sighed. "Do you want the short version or the long version?"

"I want whatever version you're willing to tell me."

She briefly thought about where to start before deciding the beginning was probably best. "Before I tell you anything, I hope you realize that I rarely share this story."

Josh clasped his hand over his heart. "I feel so honored."

Becca playfully hit his side, causing his jacket to slide slightly off her shoulder. She watched Josh's eyes glaze over the exposed skin before she lifted the jacket back in place.

"I already told you what life was like for me in high school. So when one of the more popular boys in school became interested in me and my parents got wind of it, let's just say we had no choice but to date. Since our families were friends, I'd known Rich most of my life, but he'd never seemed interested before."

"Wait," Josh said. "The judge's son is named Rich? Sounds like a jerk already."

"You have no idea," Becca said with a laugh. "By the time I was sixteen, I'd gone from a scrawny teenager to having hips and curves that got me a lot of unwanted attention. In a way, I should have known that my looks had been the turning factor for Rich. I was smart, talented and beautiful…only two of which he'd actually noticed before. My parents encouraged me to date him. Everyone did really.

"I'll spare you the details of the long, sordid saga of our high school relationship, but the reason I broke up with him was because he shared the same views as his father. He believed a woman's only place is to aid and care for her husband in any way possible. God forbid she have her own dreams and aspirations."

Josh shook his head. "I only heard the judge tell you a few choice words, but I could just imagine what type of son he has."

"And he only got worse after we broke up. He was teased in high school for being dumped by the class nerd. So in turn, he teased me about losing the best thing I ever had. Once we graduated, I'd hoped I'd never see him again, but I hadn't been so lucky. After I graduated from college, I got a high-paying corporate job downtown and, lo and behold, who started working there a week before me..."

"I hope you gave him a piece of your mind," Josh said.

"Worse. I started dating him again. Moved in with him soon after. And within a year, we were engaged to be married." Although the situation wasn't funny, Becca laughed at the surprised look on Josh's face.

"I didn't see that coming."

"Needless to say, I ended our engagement for the same reasons we broke up in high school, but this time, certain members of our community couldn't handle the fact that I'd embarrassed Rich once again. In particular, the judge and his family. Then I quit my corporate job to help Haley with The Aunt Penny Foundation. In turn, my family had to deal with a lot of gossip because of the decisions I'd made." She didn't mention how despite the fact that she'd never seen eye to eye with her parents, she felt guilty for what she'd put them through.

Josh leaned toward her and whispered in her ear. "You did the right thing, Becca. And sometimes, doing the right thing is the hardest decision of all."

Becca nodded her head, as she tried to ignore how close he was. "I know I did, but I changed after that. I've never cared what people thought of me and I promised myself after that situation that I'd never change myself for a man again. I lost a piece of myself that I'm just now starting to get back." Becca shivered when she felt the back of her hand graze his cheek.

"I never did understand a man who didn't want a woman who was his equal, but rather one who didn't have a mind of her own." His voice was even deeper than it had been previously. "If I ever marry, I need a woman who's going to challenge me in ways I've never been challenged. A woman who wants me to walk beside her as we go through life, but is independent and filled with vigor and passion."

He was so close that all Becca had to do was turn her head and their lips would be centimeters apart. Her heart was beating so fast that she couldn't hear anything else. She chanced a glance in his direction and was taken aback by the look she saw in his eyes.

"For a night that's supposed to be about business," she said, "we sure are talking about a lot of non-business-related topics."

"Is this just about business?" Josh asked. "Because this feels like a helluva lot more than just business."

She turned to him then, filled with questions that she refused to ask and answers he'd never give. *Don't get lost in those baby blues.* She wasn't sure if it was the moonlight hitting his profile perfectly or the sound of the waves crashing on the shore in the distance, but the energy around them became even more electric.

"If we take this any further, it would be wrong."

"I disagree, Ms. Wright." Josh's eyes bounced from

hers to her lips. "I think stopping here would be the real tragedy."

His lips crashed onto hers with an urgency she should have seen coming but that nearly knocked her off her feet nonetheless. His hands curled around her waist, bringing her closer to him. Her instinct was to pull away, but instead she wrapped her arms around his neck. His tongue slipped into her mouth in one full motion, methodically stroking hers. Never had she experienced a kiss so explosive. So intense.

Becca was the first to pull away.

"Wow," she said, although she hadn't meant to.

"Wow is right." Josh leaned in for a couple more pecks before he released her. If she hadn't been near the railing, she was certain her steps would have faltered.

"Maybe it's time to call it a night," she suggested. "I have an early morning tomorrow."

For a moment, she thought he was going to try to convince her to prolong the night. She was glad when he nodded his head and started walking back to the vehicle with her. They walked in silence, each consumed by their own thoughts. It wasn't until they were almost to the car that she realized he'd held her hand the entire walk back.

Chapter 8

"Mom, for the last time, nothing is going on with me and Joshua DeLong." Becca dropped her forehead into her hands as her mother rattled on about the newspaper photo.

Although Becca had enjoyed attending the movie premiere with Josh a couple nights ago, she wouldn't have been so carefree when the photographer snapped photos if she'd known they would end up in the local paper.

"Becca, you could have told your father and me that you were dating Joshua DeLong."

Clearly her mother did not get it. "Mom, like I said yesterday, Mr. DeLong is in charge of charity outreach and public relations for Prescott George, and The Aunt Penny Foundation was chosen as the recipient for their gala. We're working together and the only reason I attended the movie premiere was to network and spread the word about the foundation and gala. That's all."

"Well, sweetie, that didn't look like a photo you take with someone you just work with," her mom said. "And I talked to a few people who said you two looked rather cozy together. You could have told me you were dating him. I was going to set you up on a date with Mrs. Higgins's grandson for next week, but now I won't."

Becca had no doubt that Judge Chapmen and his associates were the "few people" who'd told her parents about how cozy she'd looked with Josh.

"And, Becca, you looked gorgeous in that photo. I've been telling you to show your curves for years and now that you have, you caught the eye of a Mogul. Oh my goodness, I can't believe it. But maybe you should invest in a better strapless bra next time. I know the perfect place…"

Becca's mind wandered as her mother continued to talk. To say her mother was excited about the possibility that Becca was dating Josh was an understatement. All Patricia Wright had been consumed with lately was marrying Becca off and marrying her off well. Josh represented everything Patricia wanted for her daughter.

"Mom, I hate to end this exciting call, but I have to go."

"I know you're being sarcastic, but okay, dear. I'll talk to you later. Maybe you could even bring Joshua DeLong by to meet your father and me sometime soon? If you're friends like you say, that would be appropriate, right?"

"Um…right." Becca walked to her kitchen to make herself a cup of French vanilla coffee. Even though she could probably use something stronger. "Okay, Mom, I love you and I'll talk to you soon."

She'd just turned on the Keurig when her phone rang again. She answered without even looking at the name of the caller.

"Mom, if you're going to ask me about Joshua De-Long again, I'm going to shut my phone off."

"Nice to hear from you too, Becca."

"Oh shoot." Becca dropped her phone on her hard-wood floor at the sound of Josh's voice. After taking a few seconds to breathe, she picked it up. "I'm sorry. I thought you were my mother."

"Let me guess. Your mother saw the photo of us in the newspaper."

"Yeah, my mother and half of Florida! My phone has been ringing constantly."

"But you saw the mention of The Aunt Penny Foundation and the gala, right? Have any calls been for donations?"

Becca sighed. She hated to admit it, but the phones at the foundation had been ringing nonstop for two days. They'd received some hefty donations as a result of the news article and the connections she'd made at the movie premiere. She'd worked practically around the clock, till Haley finally convinced her to take a day off.

"Yes," she admitted, "we've received some substantial donations. I guess now is the time where you remind me that no publicity is bad publicity?"

"I don't have to. You just did." She could almost feel him smirking through the phone.

"What can I do for you, Josh?" When he remained silent she asked, "Josh?"

"For the record," he finally said, "you should never

ask a question like that to a man who you passionately kissed and left pining for more."

Becca laughed. "I can hardly imagine you pining for anyone. But I'll rephrase the question."

"No need. I signed up for a volunteer event today and I was calling to see if you wanted to help me out. Since I know you're probably working, if you have an hour or two to spare, I'd really appreciate it. My brother Logan bailed and my other brothers are busy."

Becca glanced at her phone as if it had two heads. "Out of all the people you know, you called *me* to volunteer with you?"

"It's the least you could do since you're the one who ended our kiss," he said with a laugh. "All jokes aside, I really enjoy your company and thought it would be nice to do some volunteer work together. If you want, we can discuss the contacts we made from the movie premiere and decide our next steps."

Becca glanced around her condo and weighed her options for the day. Stay home and binge watch her favorite shows? Or spend the day with Josh doing volunteer work? Her decision was easy.

"I'm actually off today, so I can help you. What will we be doing?"

"You'll see," he said. "Wear something you don't mind getting dirty. I'll pick you up in an hour."

Becca wasn't sure there was anything more adorable than a black-and-white puppy. Except for possibly a black-and-white puppy being washed by a sexy millionaire with brilliant blue eyes.

When they'd arrived at the animal shelter to participate in a nationwide initiative to connect animals with loving families, Becca hadn't been prepared to see this side of Josh. Already, he'd played with and bathed over ten dogs and puppies before speaking with prospective families about the animals they hoped to adopt.

"Pretty hot, huh?"

Becca turned to face Tinley, one of the managers at the shelter. "Um, what do you mean?"

Tinley rolled her eyes. "Oh, come on, Becca, you know I'm talking about Josh. You haven't taken your eyes off him since you guys got here."

Becca looked down at the current ball of fur she was holding. The cat purred when Becca rubbed the top of her head. "Is it that obvious?"

"It is," Tinley said with a laugh. "But who could blame you? What woman isn't a sucker for a man with a puppy? Add Josh's handsome looks to the mix and you're a goner. But don't worry. He's been checking you out all day, too."

Becca glanced down at her yoga pants and tank that was covered in fur, and splattered with water and dirt from a dog that had been way too big for her to wash herself.

Tinley waved a finger at her. "Whatever you're thinking, stop. I know what I'm talking about. No matter how filthy you've gotten after a day of volunteering with these rascals, that man over there has had his eyes on you all day."

Becca shivered. She hadn't noticed Josh paying attention to her, but that was probably because she'd been too busy trying not to pay attention to him…and failing.

Josh glanced up then and caught her gaze. Despite the array of people and pets scattered around, they didn't break eye contact.

"Honey, Josh has been volunteering here for years and I've never seen him look at anyone the way he's looking at you."

"What about the other women he's brought here?" Becca asked without breaking eye contact.

"What women? If anything, he brings one of his brothers. Never a woman. You're the first the staff and other volunteers have met, and since that photo of you two in the paper circulated the office, we recognized you the minute you walked through the door."

Tinley proceeded to ask Becca questions about the movie premiere, but Becca barely heard her own answers. She was too busy staring back at Josh, trying to keep her heart in check.

To Josh, intelligence and beauty made a great combination in a woman. If you added feisty and willing to get her hands dirty to the mix, the combination was dangerous.

As Josh sat outside his favorite sandwich shop with Becca later that day, he reminded himself that he was supposed to be eating, not creepily watching her eat. If he hadn't been kissing those soft lips days prior, he probably would have been able to concentrate more.

"I never would have thought to put meat and lettuce on a bagel with cream cheese. It's delicious," Becca said, taking another bite of her sandwich.

He took a bite of his own sandwich, never taking his eyes off her as he did. She had a couple dirt smudges on her cheeks that he figured he should probably tell her about. But he thought they looked too adorable to wash off. It showed just how much effort she'd dedicated to the animal shelter.

"If you're going to keep staring at me, the least you could do is talk to me."

Josh mentally shook his head from its Becca-induced state. "Sorry, I was just thinking about how great you were today. You really dived right in with helping the animals and I think it's amazing that we were able to get over thirty animals adopted in a few hours."

"I had a lot of fun today! And I never would have pegged you for an animal guy."

"Oh really?" He quirked an eyebrow. "What type of guy did you have me pegged for?"

"I don't know," she said with a shrug. "I guess since you live on a yacht and you're constantly on the move, I just didn't imagine you as the type who had time for pets."

"I'll admit that I do travel a lot, but I always make time for animals. My dog, Bailey, just passed away last year, but before she did, she went everywhere with me, as long as it was dog friendly."

Becca's eyes lit up. "What type of dog was she?"

"A brown Lab. I've always had Labs, so I'm partial to them."

"I grew up with golden retrievers. The eight-week-old golden retriever I was holding today was so cute, I almost adopted him. I wasn't surprised he was one of the first to go."

"Puppies always go fast. Every time I volunteer I'm tempted to adopt one of the older dogs. I'm sure the staff is waiting for me to choose one."

"But you haven't found the perfect match?"

"Exactly. When I find my future dog, I'll know it. Until then, I find joy in helping other loving families find their perfect pet."

Becca took a sip of her water and finished off her sandwich. "Did you have anything else planned for today?"

Am I imagining it, or does she seem like she wants to spend more time with me? "This was the only thing I had planned for today. Why? Did you have any ideas?"

"No ideas. Just curious since I have the day off. We don't have to do something else, though."

Josh thought about what they could do. He didn't want to pass up an opportunity to spend more time with Becca. He had an idea. "The sun is going down soon, so we'd have to leave now. It's a little unconventional, but if you're down for a quick adventure, I'd love to show you one of my favorite spots."

"Let's go."

Josh almost dropped the rest of his sandwich at her quick response. He expected her to ask more questions. He took the rest of his sandwich to go and they made their way to his black Maserati.

"I meant to ask," she said as she sat in the car. "If you live on your yacht, where do you store your cars?"

When he'd picked up Becca to take her to the animal shelter, she'd performed her normal thorough search of his vehicle but hadn't asked any additional questions. He knew her curiosity would eventually get the best of her.

"The Moguls own their own car storage lockers, so I store all five of my cars there."

Becca lifted both eyebrows. "Five? What are the other three?"

"You'll find out one day."

She pouted and crossed her arms over her chest. "You suck."

When Josh pulled up to a red light, he glanced over

at her. "Didn't we discuss choosing your words wisely the other day?" There were a whole lot of things he wanted to suck, if only she'd give him the opportunity.

Her lips parted into a perfect O upon realizing her error. The car crackled with sexual tension until they made it to their destination. Josh pulled into his normal discreet location in a dark corner underneath a bridge. After they got out of the car, he covered the part of his car that was visible with a long piece of cardboard that was leaning against a concrete wall.

"Okay, now I'm concerned. Why are you hiding your car?"

"Shhh." He gently covered her mouth and pulled her to the side of the car. He didn't release her mouth until he was sure no one was around.

"What is going on?" she whispered. "Where are we?"

"We're at the Miami Marine Stadium. Have you heard of it?"

"Yeah. It's a historical landmark, right?"

"Right. It was created to watch speed boating back in the sixties and has been closed for decades. We're parked right behind it."

Becca lifted her head and glanced around. "I'm guessing we aren't allowed to be here."

"That assumption would be correct." Josh grabbed her hand and increased his walking speed when they were out in the open. "It's not open to the public, except for special events. Even then, you can't really get near the stadium unless you're part of the organization devoted to the historical preservation of this place."

"If we aren't allowed to be here, why are we here?"

"You'll see," he said with a smile. Making sure the

coast was clear, he walked over to the easiest wall to climb over. "Here, stand on my hands. I'll lift you over."

Becca stared at him. "You can't be serious."

"I'm dead serious." He linked his hands together. When a noise in the distance caught their attention, Josh glanced over in time to see the security guard making his rounds. "Better act fast unless you want to get arrested."

That definitely got Becca's attention. She was over the wall in no time with Josh right behind her. He led her around the side to the entrance of the stadium.

"Wow," she said, looking out over Biscayne Bay and the city of Miami. "This view is amazing."

"It is." Josh grabbed her hand and led her to a more discreet corner. "But this view is the reason I come here."

Becca gasped when Josh stood back to let her soak in the entire graffiti-covered stadium. "I've never seen anything like it."

"Pretty remarkable, right?" Josh jogged up a few steps, then turned to face her. "There isn't a part of the stadium that's not covered in graffiti. But it's not just the graffiti and breathtaking views that I love. It's the fact that the graffiti tells a story."

Becca jogged up to meet him. "How so?"

"Some of the best graffiti artists in Miami contributed to the artwork displayed across this stadium. When I was younger, my dad used to sneak here with my brothers and me and tell us stories about the famous street artists who added to the beauty of this place."

Josh started walking to the top of the stadium. "You see, most people think the graffiti destroys the beauty of the stadium, whereas my dad always taught us that the rich colors and detailed images are a form of expression that created a message that helped define this place. On days when I need a pick-me-up, I come here and soak in the inspiration that I imagine those artists felt when they created their artwork."

When he reached a private corner, he leaned against the wall. "You see, I was never good at drawing or painting. Hell, I wasn't even a good writer. But I've always been intelligent. I always saw things a little differently. Interpreted life in a way others didn't. I always felt like no one really understood the world like I understood it…except my brother Logan, although I'd never tell him that. Being here with my father always made me feel like I belonged to something greater than what people expected of me. In a way, I guess I still feel that way when I come here."

Josh had been so wrapped up in the memories he had here with his father that he hadn't noticed how Becca was closely observing him. "What? Do I have something on my face?"

Becca smiled. "You joke around when you get nervous, don't you?"

"Baby, Joshua DeLong—brilliant corporate raider—never gets nervous."

Becca leaned her body into his, pushing him closer against the wall than he already was. "That may be true. But Josh DeLong—the man who volunteers at an animal shelter, takes long walks in the park to think and reminisces about precious moments in a graffiti-stricken stadium—does get nervous." He swallowed the sudden lump in his throat.

"I like this side of you," she said right before her lips met his. When she'd pushed him against the wall, he should have been prepared for her boldness, but he hadn't been. After the kiss they'd shared a few days ago, all Josh had been able to think about was kissing her again.

He tried to will his hands to stay by his sides, but they somehow made their way to her backside, pulling her even closer to him than she already was. Her lips were intoxicating and her sweet moans filling the warm air were enough to increase his boldness.

He wanted to let her hair out of her high ponytail so that he could embed his fingers in it, but he settled for sliding them underneath her shirt instead. Josh ran one of his hands up the side of her body before palming one breast and teasing her nipple through her thin bra. She shuddered beneath his fingers when he tweaked the other nipple.

Kissing Becca was unlike anything he'd experienced before. He'd always liked the art of kissing, but with Becca, he found the act even more enjoyable. The way their tongues tangled in perfect unison caused lust-filled groans to erupt from deep within him. He could have stood there kissing her forever, but at the sound of someone clearing their throat, they broke apart.

Becca stared up at him with wide eyes, clearly assuming security had just spotted them. When Josh glanced over Becca's shoulder, he frowned.

"What are you doing here?"

"I should be asking you the same question."

Becca slowly turned around to see who he was talking to before glancing back at Josh. Josh made sure her shirt was in place before walking her over. "Becca, I'd like for you to meet my brother Logan. Logan, this is Becca." He was sure his brother had seen them kissing, but even if he hadn't, her swollen lips would have given them away.

"Nice to meet you," Becca said, shaking his hand.

"The pleasure's all mine." When Logan kissed the back of Becca's hand, Josh gave Logan a look that warned him to tread carefully.

"I thought you had something to do today, little brother."

Logan laughed. "I finished early. When I went by the shelter, they said you'd already left. Clearly you found a better replacement."

Becca smiled, already falling for the Logan charm. Logan winked at Josh, obviously enjoying the fact that he'd interrupted Josh's time with Becca.

"So what are you doing here?" Josh asked. Just then, a noise sounded from the corner. All three of them turned to face a woman approaching. She was adjusting her short dress and wig, and wearing entirely too much makeup.

"He's here with me," she said as she grabbed Logan's arm. Josh had to stifle a laugh.

"Josh and Becca, this is Trina," Logan said.

"That's not my name," the woman said. "Try again."

Logan snapped his fingers. "Sorry, it's Tracy, right?"

"Nope." She crossed her arms over her ample chest that was spilling out of her dress. "Try again."

"That's right," Logan said, hitting his head. "It's Tamika. How could I forget?"

"Logannnn," she whined. "My name doesn't even begin with a *T*."

Josh rolled his eyes and leaned over to Becca. "We could be here all night."

Becca's laughter filled the air, but didn't distract

Logan and the woman whose name he still hadn't figured out.

"How about we head back to my yacht?" Josh suggested in a low voice as he kissed the side of her neck. "Maybe talk business."

"Talk business? I don't believe you. I refuse to be another notch on your belt," she said. "And The Aunt Penny Foundation is too important to me."

"You wouldn't be," he whispered. "But I love a challenge, so if you want to stay here with my brother and his flavor of the day, how about we take bets on how many tries it will take for him to get her name right."

Becca smiled. "You're on."

As they placed their bets, Josh thought about both the kisses he'd shared with Becca. He couldn't blame her for turning down his offer to go back to his yacht. He didn't even trust that he could keep it strictly business if he had her anywhere near a bed. They were supposed to be working together, but he couldn't remember the last time he'd worked with someone whom he constantly wanted to touch…and kiss.

Unfortunately, the fact that she'd turned him down only made him want her more. After two kisses, he was already addicted to Becca's taste and he feared that as time went on, his craving for her would only get worse. *You're in trouble, DeLong, and this time, trouble is in the form of a woman named Becca Wright.*

Chapter 9

"Becca, can you please stop fidgeting with your dress?" Haley asked after Becca tugged at her sleek black dress for the fifth time since they'd exited the car.

"I can't help it. I'm nervous."

Haley laughed. "I never thought I'd see the day when you got nervous over a meeting. Usually you're so composed."

"Yeah, well, usually I haven't made out a couple times with one of the men we're giving a presentation to."

Becca and Haley had been invited to attend the monthly meeting of Prescott George in Miami's financial district to discuss the goals of The Aunt Penny Foundation and how the Millionaire Moguls might be able to join forces with them in a more permanent manner. This meeting was a huge opportunity for Becca and

Haley, but the only thing Becca could think about was ways to calm her rattled nerves.

Haley raised a finger in the air. "Have I mentioned how proud I am of you? Making out with a man who was featured on the cover of a national business magazine as one of the most influential black men in America is not an easy feat, my dear. Yet you made it look easy."

"I'm definitely not making it look easy now." Becca tugged at her dress again. She had to admit, it was nice to feel a little like her old self, and now that she was back to wearing heels her calves felt amazing. Yet despite how great she felt, her stomach was doing somersaults at the idea that she was going to see Josh after basically throwing herself at him days prior.

As they approached a tall older tower, they slowed their stride. Haley glanced at the sheet of paper in her hand. "Are we sure this is the Prescott George headquarters? There's nothing indicating that the Millionaire Moguls are located here."

"I recall Josh saying that they don't advertise the headquarters. They prefer not to draw attention to anything that may happen behind closed doors."

Haley shrugged. "That makes sense. Is there a secret code we have to enter in order to cross the premises?"

"Something like that," Becca said with a laugh. She glanced up at the tower and took a deep breath.

Haley lightly shook Becca's shoulders. "You'll be fine. I'm sure the Moguls will have many other things on their minds besides paying attention to us until it's time for our presentation… Josh included!"

Becca rolled her neck. "You're right. I can do this. Let's go."

After following the directions to enter the building, as promised, Josh was waiting exactly where he said he would be. The minute her eyes landed on him, her heartbeat quickened.

"Hello, Becca." Her name rolled off his tongue.

"Hello, Josh." His black Ray-Bans were pushed back on top of his head and he was wearing navy blue slacks and a gray shirt that was unbuttoned at the top. He had that I-look-this-good-without-trying sort of thing going on that made her clench her thighs as much as she could while standing. When Haley nudged her, she snapped out of her Josh-induced fog.

"Joshua DeLong, I'd like for you to meet the founder of The Aunt Penny Foundation, Haley Adams. Haley, this is Joshua DeLong."

After they finished with the pleasantries, Joshua led them into a long, dimly lit hallway. The walls were adorned with vintage black-and-white photographs of men who Becca assumed had something to do with the organization. It was hard not to stare at the eyes gazing down at her from the walls.

"Don't stare too hard," Josh said, flashing her a pearly-white smile. "These walls represent Prescott George's history, and rumor has it if you stare too hard into the eyes of a founder, you'll begin to think the photograph is really staring back at you."

Becca laughed it off. "Yeah, right." She was still thinking about Josh's words when they entered a large room. At first glance, it looked like an old boy's club with wood paneling and leather furniture as the main decor. To Becca, the room screamed old money. On one wall, there were floor-to-ceiling glass shelves covered with bottles of Scotch. On another wall sat rows and rows of books that Becca wished she could take a peek at. In the center of the room was a large unlit fireplace. But what really got her attention was the group of men clustered around it. All of them oozed richness and power, even as they stared at her and Haley as if they were the main attraction.

"I take that back," Haley whispered. "They may have been discussing important Mogul business, but we have definitely captured their attention."

Becca swallowed. Seeing a group of men like the Moguls all in one room was intimidating and intriguing all at the same time. As Josh introduced them, she noted that each man either welcomed them, gave them a nod or raised their glass. Then, as quickly as they'd become the center of attention, suddenly they weren't.

"Well, that was nerve-racking," Haley said.

"They're all harmless," Josh said with a laugh. "Right now, I'm sure they're all taking bets on the latest sports game. Usually, if the Moguls each have a Scotch in their hand, we're almost finished discussing business. Back in the day, smoking stogies would have been an indicator."

Becca noticed Josh stiffen when his eyes caught someone over her shoulder. She turned to the man as he approached.

"Ladies, my name is Ashton Rollins and I'm the president of Prescott George. I'd like to thank you for accepting our meeting invitation and congratulate you on being chosen as the charity recipient for this year's gala."

"Thank you." Becca shook Ashton's hand. After several moments, she cleared her throat when Haley didn't speak up.

"Thank you," Haley finally said. Haley was still staring at Ashton as he walked away. When she looked back at Becca, all Becca could do was smile. In all honesty, she understood the effect that Ashton had on Haley. Josh had the same effect on her.

"Okay," Josh said, getting their attention. "In about five minutes, you two will give your presentation on The Aunt Penny Foundation. I've talked about the foundation at length, but nothing is as good as hearing the details from the horse's mouth. Let your passion seep through your words and I'm sure all the members will see what I've been saying for weeks."

Becca looked at him expectantly. "And what have you been saying?"

Josh searched her eyes, briefly dropping his gaze to her lips. "That The Aunt Penny Foundation was created by extremely talented and passionate women who are determined to make a difference in the community by giving less fortunate students a chance to go to college—an opportunity they otherwise wouldn't have. They know you're both amazing. You just have to prove to them *how* amazing."

Although the foundation had a lot riding on this meeting, Becca's mind was frazzled with thoughts of the man staring back at her. When they'd first met, it had seemed as if he was always saying the wrong thing. Now she felt like he was always saying the right thing.

His jaw clenched and she noticed he also squeezed his fists together at his sides. *I wonder if he's having as hard a time keeping his hands off me as I am keeping mine off him.*

Becca thought back to a conversation she, Haley and a couple other girlfriends had had in college. Becca had teased one of their friends who'd claimed that a guy in her English class was so sexy, she could "jump his bones." Having never experienced the feeling herself, it had been easy to make fun of the statement. But back then, she hadn't known Joshua DeLong. Now that she did, she wished she'd listened to the women as they'd given tips and tricks on keeping their womanly urges under control. She'd need every one of them to resist this sexy man.

"Earth to Becca," Haley whispered. "Would you get a room already?"

At Josh's smile, Becca immediately closed her eyes. She didn't know what was worse: the fact that Haley was right—all she wanted to do was drag Josh to the nearest empty room and make sweet love to him—or the fact that Josh had obviously heard Haley's bad rendition of a whisper. Becca sighed. *This is going to be the longest presentation of my life.*

A chime echoing throughout the room caused her to open her eyes.

"It's time," Josh said as he led them through a side door to a conference room. Becca and Haley took a couple seats at the end of the front row as Josh went to the podium to make introductions. Once they were seated Haley's phone chimed, indicating that she had a text message.

"You need to shut off your phone," Becca whispered.

"Sorry." Haley grabbed her phone out of her purse and read the message. Seconds later, the handbag tipped off her lap, spilling a few items onto the floor. When Becca glanced at her, all color was drained from Haley's face.

Becca touched her shoulder and spoke in a low voice. "Hales, what is it? Is everything okay?"

"No, it's not. Aunt Penny has been taken to the hospital. My parents don't know what's wrong yet." Haley was on the brink of tears as she gathered her fallen items. She showed Becca the text message when she leaned over to help her. The text was cryptic, but it didn't sound good.

"Oh my goodness, let's go. I'll drive your car to the hospital."

"No, you can't do that," Haley whispered. "The foundation has a lot riding on this presentation. You stay here and I'll call you as soon as I know more."

"No, Haley. Let me come with you." Becca glanced around to make sure no one could hear them. "It's Aunt Penny. We have to check on her."

Haley spoke a little more sternly. "This is a once-in-a-lifetime meeting. I need you to get up there and give a presentation that will wow the Moguls so much, they'll support The Aunt Penny Foundation past the gala. I need you, Becca."

Becca's own eyes were filling with tears, but she shook them off. "Okay, you go and I'll stay here. But the minute you know more, promise you'll tell me."

"I promise." Haley made a quick exit just as Josh called them to take the stage. Becca appreciated the applause; it concealed the loud sigh that had escaped her lips when she rose from her seat. She ignored the concerned look on Josh's face when she approached the podium. *Now isn't the time to get frazzled, Becca. Now is the time to deliver.* She may have been upset. She may have wished she was headed to see Aunt Penny instead of giving this presentation. However, she'd never let Haley down. Haley, Aunt Penny and the foundation needed her to step up now more than ever.

Becca was the consummate professional. There was no other way to put it. She was delivering a presentation worthy of a roomful of millionaires, yet Josh could tell that something was wrong. He doubted any of the Moguls could detect her emotions, but he noticed the tension in her posture and the stress lines in her forehead.

When her presentation ended, the men gave her a standing ovation. Josh didn't miss the appreciative glances that some of the men were shooting her way. He couldn't blame them. She looked beautiful in her sleek black dress and black heels. Her hair, free and flowing around her shoulders, looked just as striking as it had the last time he'd seen her.

Every time a Mogul approached her, Becca politely smiled, but her eyes were screaming a different message: *I need to leave and I need to leave now.*

"Are you okay?" Josh asked when he was able to corner her alone.

She shook her head. "No, I'm not okay. Right before the presentation, Haley got a message that Aunt Penny was rushed to the hospital. I don't have any more information and all I want to do is take a cab out of here, but this meeting is important to us."

Josh was already shaking his head. "Your presentation went great. You've done what you came here to do. Let me drive you to the hospital."

Becca nodded her head. "Okay. Thank you."

"Stay here and I'll be right back." Josh searched the room for Daniel Cobb. They'd been playing phone tag for days and lately it had been more apparent than ever that Prescott George was stuck in the Dark Ages. Daniel and Josh were finally supposed to talk to a few other members about the direction of Prescott George.

He spotted Daniel talking with Ashton. *Crap.* There was no way he could pull Daniel aside with Ashton right there. Although it had been over a month, Josh still recalled his argument with Ashton about the way the organization handled charity outreach and public relations. He didn't need a repeat performance, especially when Becca needed him.

Deciding he'd just text Daniel later, Josh walked back over to Becca and led her out of the building and to his car.

"Do you know what hospital Aunt Penny is at?"

"Yeah, Haley texted me when she arrived." Becca showed him the message. Josh typed the address into his GPS and then placed a hand over Becca's.

"It's going to be okay. Don't worry."

"You don't understand," Becca said as her voice cracked with emotion. "Aunt Penny is more than just the name behind the foundation. I know I told you what she means to Haley, but she means a lot to me, too. Although I love my family, my relationship with my parents has always seemed to have strings attached. When Haley and I became roommates in college and I had the pleasure of meeting Aunt Penny, I felt like all of a sudden I had my own personal cheerleader."

Josh glanced at Becca to make sure she was still holding up okay. "Maybe you would feel better if you called Haley and told her you were on your way."

"That's a good idea." Becca dialed Haley and didn't relax her shoulders until she heard Haley's voice.

"Everything went great. Josh is bringing me to the

hospital right now." Becca frowned. "Haley, I want to be there. You shouldn't have to go through this alone."

Josh squeezed her hand for support. It was difficult knowing what she needed when he could only hear one side of the conversation.

"Okay, Hales. I love you and I'm here for you if you need anything. Keep me in the loop." Becca placed her phone in her lap and sighed. "They don't know much about Aunt Penny's current condition, but for now she can't have any visitors. Haley is there with her parents. She says she's okay and she'll call me if anything changes."

Josh just kept driving while Becca gathered her thoughts. He hated seeing her look so helpless. "Do you want me to take you home?"

She didn't look his way when she spoke. "If you don't mind, that would be great."

There's nothing I'd mind doing for you. He didn't dare say the words that were floating around in his head. "I don't mind at all," he said instead.

Josh turned his car around to head in the direction of Becca's home. He took her lead and remained silent the entire drive there, never removing his free hand from hers.

Chapter 10

"Is it okay if I walk you to your door?" Josh asked after he pulled into a parking space in her lot.

Becca looked from her complex to Josh. "Actually, if it isn't too much trouble, would you mind coming up for a while? I could make us some tea."

Josh ran the back of his hand down her cheek. "Sure."

Normally, Becca would never have invited Josh up to her cute one-bedroom condo in the middle-class Floridian neighborhood. It wasn't that she was ashamed of where she lived. Quite the opposite. Whether Josh was a millionaire or not, she was proud of her condo and the neighborhood she lived in.

It was just that there was something extremely personal about inviting him into her home. Had she not been so upset over Aunt Penny, she probably would have thought twice about it.

"Here we are," she said, opening her door. Josh stepped through the threshold of her humble abode. After growing up in a house with entirely too many rooms, she'd been happy to trade it in for a quaint condo suitable for one. Despite the smaller space, her contemporary decor, open floor plan and multiuse furnishing made her home appear much larger than it was.

Josh ran his fingers over the white marble island in her kitchen. "I really love your style. Reminds me a lot of the type of decor I have throughout my yacht."

"Based on what I saw on the first deck, I can definitely see the resemblance."

"I'll have to give you a full tour next time." Josh glanced at her chic coffee-colored couch. "Tell you what. How about you take a seat and I'll make us both some tea. Sound good?"

"You're a guest. I should be the one making you a cup of tea."

Josh smiled. "I'm sure I can manage. You've had an emotional evening, so you should rest." At the reminder of Aunt Penny, Becca's eyes watered.

"I'm so sorry. I shouldn't have said anything to remind you about the situation."

"It's not your fault. I'll probably be thinking about Aunt Penny all night. That's why I wish I could have gone to the hospital with Haley when she got the news."

Becca connected her phone to her Bluetooth speaker in her living room, closing her eyes when smooth neo soul music filled her condo. At the sound of the boiling water whistling, she turned to Josh. His eyes met hers with laser focus. She only exhaled when he broke his stare to make their tea. He opened a couple cabinets and successfully located two mugs, tea bags and honey.

"How many teaspoons of honey would you like?"

"Two, please."

When he joined her on the couch, his arm brushed against hers in a way that made her glad she was tightly gripping her mug. Otherwise she would have spilled tea over her sofa cushions.

"Stop feeling guilty," he said. "There's nothing for you to feel guilty about. From what I heard in the car, it sounds like Haley wanted you to stay and give the presentation."

"She did, but I still can't help but feel guilty." Becca took a sip of her tea. "I've had loved ones in the hospital before, but never someone as close to me as Aunt Penny is."

"I hate hospitals," Josh said as he took a sip of his own tea. "The waiting. The nervousness. Sitting in a waiting room while someone is in surgery is like the calm before the storm."

"Oh, I'm sorry." Becca placed her hand on Josh's forearm. "Talking about Aunt Penny is probably bringing up thoughts about your father, right?"

"Actually, I lost my grandfather a few years ago, so I was thinking about him this time."

"Were you close to him?"

"Extremely. He was my dad's father and after my dad passed away, my grandfather became everything to my brothers and me. Because I was the oldest grandson, he made sure that I understood what it meant to be a DeLong. Even though he was one of the best men I knew, he was also one of the most stubborn. The old man didn't even go to the doctor until he was good and ready. By that point, his time was near."

Becca scooted closer to Josh. "I'm so sorry to hear

that. Both my grandfathers passed away before I was born and I barely knew my grandmothers."

"Talking about my father's death is still difficult to me, but my grandfather was in his mid-nineties when he passed, so he lived a full life and he got to see my career take off."

"You fight hard for them, don't you?" Becca asked. "You don't say much about them, but when you do, there's a noticeable amount of pride in your voice."

"You're right," Josh said with a smile. "I told my father and grandfather that I would always honor the DeLong name. They were such admirable men, and I wanted to do something to make them both proud."

Becca leaned her head against Josh's broad shoulder, careful not to spill her tea. "With everything you've accomplished, I'm sure you've made them both extremely proud. They may not be here on earth, but they are looking down on you…celebrating your accomplishments alongside you."

"I miss them every day." Becca leaned her head up when Josh began rolling up his sleeve. "I got this infinity tattoo when my dad got sick, but it's fitting for both of them. I wanted my dad to know that no matter what happened, our bond would never be broken, whether he was here on earth…or in the afterlife."

"It's beautiful." Becca touched his bicep. "What about your mother's parents?"

Josh frowned and rolled down his sleeve before taking another sip of his tea. *Must be a touchy subject.* "They're still living."

Becca glanced at Josh, expecting him to say more. After thirty seconds of silence, she realized he wasn't going to continue. Her thoughts wandered back to Aunt Penny.

"Aunt Penny's getting up there in age, so times like these really put life into perspective. She was so looking forward to Prescott George's gala next month... What will we do if she doesn't make it?"

"You can't think like that. Even though dealing with the passing of my father and grandfather was the most difficult thing I've ever had to go through, I never gave up hope." He lightly kissed the top of her head. "And you can't, either."

"I know you're right. I think I'm exhausted since I've been working so much lately. I just need to relax my brain and stop worrying. Everything is going to be fine." Becca tried not to think too hard about the fact that she was clinging to his shirt as he held her.

"I have an idea." He grabbed both of her hands and turned her toward him. "Let's send some positive vibes Aunt Penny's way. First, close your eyes."

Becca did as he asked. "Okay, they're closed."

"Good. Now, in your mind, think of all the fun things you want to do with Aunt Penny when she gets out of the hospital and all the great things you want to update her on. Think about all the good food she'll probably want to eat when she's out of the hospital."

"Collard greens," Becca said with a laugh. "She loves collard greens and cottage cheese."

"Um, mixed together?"

Becca peeked an eye open in time to see a look of disgust cross Josh's face. "Yes, mixed together and dosed with a lot of black pepper. Need me to imagine something tastier instead?"

"While I personally may be a little sick after that description, we're talking about Aunt Penny, not me."

Becca laughed louder than she had all night. She kept her eyes open as he continued. "So think about Aunt Penny and her love for collard greens mixed with cottage cheese and topped with black pepper and then ask yourself one question…"

Becca nodded her head when he stopped talking. "And that question would be?"

"Would Aunt Penny want you to worry?"

Becca sighed. "Probably not."

"Exactly. She'd probably reprimand you for worrying about her. And then," he said, leaning slightly closer to her, "she'd make you explain how you managed to keep a rather charming and sexy man in your apartment all night without making a move on him, especially when he was wearing his lucky blue underwear."

Becca was laughing so hard tears were forming in the corners of her eyes. "How exactly would Aunt Penny know you had on your lucky underwear?"

"Didn't you know? She knows everything. Mark my words, woman. She's psychic. And in case you didn't know, she has a foundation named after her and everything, so I wouldn't doubt Aunt Penny. I hear she's a pretty remarkable woman."

By the time they finished working through random Aunt Penny scenarios, Becca was feeling lighter than she had all day.

"Josh, thank you for helping me through this." She wiped the corners of her eyes that were watery from all the laughing. "When I woke up today, the only thing that was important to me was getting through that presentation and representing The Aunt Penny Foundation to the best of my ability." *And trying not to pass out from seeing you after those explosive kisses that we shared.*

She grew more serious. "But over the course of the last few hours, everything has seemed a lot more uncertain… In all honesty, I've felt uncertain about a lot of things for a while and considering I'm known for always having the answers, I can't fathom the idea that I no longer have answers to give."

Josh lightly touched her chin so that she was looking into his bottomless blue eyes. "That's because no one has all the answers, Becca. Life is uncertain, and at times it can be more messy and unpredictable than we'd like. But the key isn't to hit those curveballs out of the park. The key is being able to understand how you hit the next ball after the curveball is thrown."

"That's the problem," Becca said. "I'm the type of person who likes to know what's coming before it actually happens, and lately I feel like I never know what's waiting around the corner."

"But that's the beauty of life." Josh's eyes briefly dropped to her lips. "Although you may not know what obstacles are waiting around the corner for you, part of the joy is that you never know what good surprises await you, either."

Becca sucked in a breath as she looked at Josh with a new pair of eyes. *He's one of the surprises I never saw coming.* Had anyone told her last month that she'd finally meet a man who made her body quiver at his touch and her heart beat faster when he said her name, she wouldn't have believed them. Yet here she was, sitting next to Joshua DeLong, craving him with a rawness that would scare her if she allowed her brain to decipher her feelings.

In the time they'd known each other, she'd already confided in him things about herself that she never thought she'd share. In turn, he'd opened up to her in ways she hadn't thought possible for the type of man that was described in all the articles she'd read about him.

To her peers, she was the nerd. The smart one. The girl who always thought she was right and the one voted most likely to run the world one day. To her parents, she was their acclaimed violinist. Their debutante. A doting wife and loving mother in the making.

To the foundation, she was the lifeline. The saving grace. The one with the connections and networking capabilities to save the place so many less fortunate students relied on to get them to college. And to herself, she was all of the above and more. She was her own worst critic. She fought so hard to be an individual and never compromise her character for anyone, yet over the years she'd managed to put more pressure on herself than anyone else had. To Becca, if people thought you were the best, then you had to be the best. Period.

Yet when she looked into Josh's eyes like she was in this moment, she didn't think about any of that. She didn't think about being a nerd or a trophy wife. She didn't see herself as an overachiever or perfectionist. Nope. The look she saw in his eyes when he stared at her like this was the type of passionate look a man gave a woman when all his lust-induced thoughts finally came to the surface. And he wasn't alone in his feelings. Becca wanted him with a fierceness that scared her. If he was the surprise that was waiting around the corner, then she was ready to turn that corner, collect her prize and never look in the other direction again.

Becca opened her mouth to speak her desires, but it was no use. Josh's lips collided with hers in a passionate kiss that stole her breath away. Unlike their previous kisses, his lips now touched hers in a way that made her wonder if he was secretly telepathic and had heard all the words she hadn't voiced out loud.

Every part of her body came alive during their kiss. Every stoke of his tongue burned her in a way that made her ache in places she'd never ached before. She wanted more. Needed more. Her teeth ran over his bottom lip when he pulled his mouth away to look at her. Through ragged breaths, she tried to concentrate on what he was saying.

"Are you sure?" he asked, his fingers tunneling in her hair.

Am I sure? Is he really asking me that? "I'm sure." When he didn't move back to kiss her, she noticed he was still observing her. Instead of spending more time talking, Becca reached her hand in between their bodies and began stroking him through his pants. The louder he groaned, the bolder her strokes got.

"Is this your way of confirming that you're sure?"

She nipped his bottom lip and increased the tempo of her strokes even more. "What do you think?"

His eyes turned from their normal color to an even darker shade of blue. She had a feeling she was about to find out exactly what he thought.

Chapter 11

Josh threw his head back to the couch and let out a groan that even he didn't recognize. He could barely think while Becca was stroking her hands up and down his length. He'd agreed to come up to her place so that he could make her feel better about Aunt Penny. As much as he wanted to drag her to her bedroom, he really needed to make sure she was on board with the sudden shift in their relationship.

"Becca," he said when she slipped her hand in his pants. "I just need to ask you one more time. Are you okay with this?" He lifted his head from the couch so that he could stare at her. When his eyes reached hers, the sly look on her face wasn't what he was expecting.

"If you're worried that I'm making a rash decision based on the emotional turn my day took when I received the news about Aunt Penny, then don't." She removed her hand from his pants and straddled him. "I know *exactly* what I'm doing and I'm sure you want it as badly as I do."

More, Josh thought. *I definitely want it more.* "I do, Becca. Trust me, I do." He'd planned on saying more, but she chose that moment to slide even farther up his body, her dress pushing higher up her golden-mocha thighs. His hands couldn't resist her bare skin.

"Stopping here would be a real tragedy." When her sweet mouth whispered the same words he'd whispered to her the night of the movie premiere, he lost the little shred of self-control he'd been holding on to. He wrapped both hands around her waist and lifted her off the couch so that they were both standing. Had she not said those words to him in such a sexy voice, he probably would have walked them both to her bedroom. But his patience was gone.

Josh grabbed the throw off the couch and spread it onto the hardwood floor in her living room.

"What are you doing?" she asked when he tossed three pillows onto the blanket.

"Do you really want to know what I'm doing?" he asked as his hands made their way to the side zipper of her dress.

"Yes," she said breathlessly, lifting her arms to give him better access.

Josh cocked his lips to the side in a grin. "What happened to that sex kitten who was just straddling me on the couch?"

"She's still here. She just wants to know what you're doing."

Josh ignored her statement and instead slid her black dress down her shoulders until it hit the floor.

She kicked the dress to the side, still wearing her black heels. Her boldness only made him devour her even more with his eyes. *Damn.* "You're breathtaking."

As he'd suspected, she was curvy in all the right places with a round butt that he couldn't wait to squeeze. Instead of black lingerie like he'd assumed, she was wearing all-white panties and a matching bra. Both were lace. Both were sexy. Both were see-through. Josh looked to the ceiling and pointed one finger in the air as he sent a silent thank-you to the love gods for blessing Becca with curves that he had no doubt would stay on his mind long after this night.

When her fingers made their way to his shirt, he was proud of the amount of restraint he had as he let her *slowly* unbutton each button. She pushed his shirt off his shoulders after the task was complete.

"Very nice," she said as she ran her hands over his abs. She glanced at him in between stroking his abs. The lust he saw in her eyes let him know that he had to act fast with his next task, before she got restless. Sure, he was dying to make long sweet love to her, but there was something that he had to do first. Something he'd been wanting to do since their first meeting.

Josh was prepared for Becca to ask more questions when his hands made their way to the rim of her panties. To his surprise, she stepped closer to him and placed a soft kiss on his jaw. With expert hands, he slid her panties down her legs and allowed his fingers to slide back up, stopping when he reached her smooth surface.

His eyes went to her face and he lifted an eyebrow. Josh knew a fresh bikini wax when he felt one and based off the sly smile Becca was giving him, he suspected that she'd done this for him. *She could be the death of me.*

He dipped his finger into her core at the same time that he kissed her with all the built-up tension he'd been feeling since their first kiss. She kissed him back with just as much passion, moaning into his mouth when his fingers began moving in and out of her. He swallowed her moans, relishing the fact that he was causing her so much pleasure.

After a few more strokes of his fingers, he released her, only long enough for her to stretch out on the throw. He joined her there, leaned back on one of the pillows and placed the other two on either side of his head. Then he dragged her body up his until she was positioned right near where he wanted her.

"Josh, what are you—" Whatever Becca had been about to say was cut off when Josh clasped his hands over each of her thighs and pulled her even farther until she was hovering over his mouth.

"Place your knees on the pillows," Josh instructed without releasing her thighs. "And place your hands on either side of you on the floor."

"Um, Josh. Are you sure you—"

Becca's words died on her lips when Josh plunged his tongue into her core. Josh felt her tense beneath his hands and tongue. "Relax, Becca," he said in between licks. "Just sit back and enjoy the ride...literally."

His tongue swirled around her clit as his hands locked her in place. After a few moments, he felt her relax and the tension in her thighs release. That was his cue to go to work.

"I've been waiting to taste your sweet nectar since you first showed up on my yacht," he said.

"You're lying." She moaned. "You didn't seem attracted to me that first day."

"Quite the contrary, Ms. Wright. I was dying to know what the buttoned-up PR director would look like if she undid a few buttons."

She laughed, but it was strained. "So you've wanted to do this for a while?"

"More than you could ever know." Josh scooted her even closer to his mouth, teasing her clit with his breath before sucking the nub into his mouth again. Then he angled her in a way that allowed him to plunge one finger into her as he dipped his tongue even farther. Soon, Becca began moving her hips to the rhythm of his tongue, her whimpers bouncing off the walls and serenading his ears.

"That feels so good," she said in a voice that was more high-pitched than it had been all night. He didn't respond for fear of breaking the good rhythm they had going. When Josh had first met Becca, he wouldn't have pegged her as a screamer. Now that he'd gotten to know her, he wasn't so sure that assumption had been correct.

"Josh," she squealed. It didn't take long for her to ride his face in the same erotic way she would move had she been riding his shaft instead. He liked her this way. Uninhibited. Unrestrained. *Unbuttoned.* Becca had been surprising him since the moment they met and now that he finally had her right where he wanted her, there was no way he was passing up the opportunity to make the most of the night.

He removed his finger from her core and moved his hands from her thighs to her butt. From there, he pushed her even farther onto his face and curled his tongue. He felt her whole body tense right before she cried in a passionate release, clenching her thighs so hard, he thought he may have to remind her that his head was still nestled between her sweetness.

After her body stopped convulsing, he felt her slide to the floor. He released her, stood up and scooped her up in his arms. She curled her head into the crook of his neck, panting in a way that a woman would after she'd had the type of orgasm Becca just experienced.

Since he wasn't sure how long it had been since she'd last had an orgasm, the right thing to do would be to give her some time to come down from her passionate high. But Josh wasn't going to do that. He wasn't done with her yet, nor did he pride himself on always doing the right thing. He liked to take chances. He liked to be reckless. And right now, he wanted to continue his reckless night with Becca and not listen to the voice that was warning him that she wasn't the type of woman that a man had sex with and forgot about. She was the type that tended to be a game changer.

The coolness of her cotton sheets grazed Becca's body when Josh laid her down on her bed. After having such a strong orgasm in her living room, she felt weak. It'd been years since she'd experienced an orgasm like the one Josh had provided for her.

The music from her living room was still drifting through her condo. Her eyes went to Josh, who was circling her bed like a vulture waiting to swoop down on its prey. He was still wearing his pants, but his abs were on full display, taunting her, causing her body to tingle.

His hands moved to the waistband of his pants, and in one calculated move he removed them along with his boxers. Becca felt as though she were watching a striptease. All that was missing was Josh busting out a few moves after he'd removed his clothes.

However, what truly captivated her complete attention was the elongated piece of equipment that was staring her in the face from her position on the bed. *It's beautiful.* There really wasn't another word for it.

"Like what you see?"

She licked her lips. "Tonight is giving me more pleasure than my modest toy collection ever did." Her hands flew to her mouth. *Please tell me I did not just say that out loud!* One look at Josh let her know that she wasn't that lucky.

"Toys, huh? I didn't peg you as the adult toy type."

"Well, I'm sure there are a lot of things about me that you didn't expect." She extended her legs, giving him a better view of her nearly naked body, as if to prove her point.

His eyes roamed over her, leaving a fiery path in their wake. She felt alive in every place his eyes touched. When their eyes connected, he squinted. "Show me."

"Show you what?"

"Your *modest* collection."

Her eyes widened. "You want me to show you my toy collection?"

"Yes." His voice was hoarse. Direct. Josh always seemed confident, but standing there in front of her, sexy and naked, she would have expected some of his cockiness to wear off. Instead, he seemed more self-assured than ever. *Now's not the time to clam up, Becca.* She'd come this far; no way she could stop now.

She stood up, clad in only her white lace bra, and walked over to her closet. She could feel Josh's eyes on her the entire time, but to his credit, he stood there, awaiting her return. When she reached her closet, she pulled the black velvet box from her shelf and placed it on the bed.

"Open it," Josh directed.

Becca untied the ribbon that was securing it in place and opened the box, revealing at least seven toys, in addition to sex dice, couples' playing cards and furry handcuffs.

Josh quirked an eyebrow as he picked up the handcuffs. "So I guess you tried all this stuff before."

Hmm, is that a hint of jealousy I hear in his voice?

"Actually, I haven't. But I've always had a bit of an infatuation with creative lovemaking. So I wanted to be prepared in case I ever met someone willing to try any of it. My exes were never explorers in the bedroom." *Good job, Becca. Why don't you continue to advertise your sad love life to the sexiest man you've ever met?*

"I was hoping you'd say that." A cheeky grin spread across his face. "What's your favorite toy to use?"

Without hesitation, she picked up her purple vibrator. "Hands down, this is my favorite and one of the few I've used."

He took the vibrator out of her hand and put the rest of the box on the floor. "Scoot higher on the bed and lie back." He picked up his discarded pants and grabbed a condom from his wallet before joining her on the bed. Once settled between her legs, he reached for the front clasp of her bra and released her breasts. They sprung free and her nipples immediately peaked under his piercing stare.

Josh wasted no time sucking a nipple into his hot mouth while his fingers played with the nipple of her other breast. Her back rose off the bed at the sensations shooting through her as a result of his mouth and hands. She was so wrapped up in pleasure, she didn't notice that her vibrator had joined the mix until she focused on the slight buzzing noise in the room.

She thought he was going to ask what type of vibrator it was. She knew there had been no need when she felt the vibrator slide into her, the tip teasing her clit. Josh had figured out how to use it more quickly than she had. Soon her muffled moans joined the buzzing sound and she was moving her hips against the device. Having the vibrator inside her while Josh's tongue and fingers played with her nipples was enough to bring her over the edge a second time tonight. When she was seconds away from another orgasm, Josh removed the vibrator, embedding himself deep within her in its place.

"Ahh!" Becca cried aloud at the level of completeness she had with him inside her. She hadn't even felt him put on the condom, but a quick glance at their connecting bodies proved that he had.

"That feels so good," she said as she adjusted to his size.

"You feel amazing." His deep voice filled her ears in a way that made her increase the movement of her hips. Soon, Josh added the vibrator again, only this time, he used it to intensify the pleasure of her breasts. She was vaguely aware that her bedroom light was still on. Luckily for her, it gave her a much better view of just how close Josh was to the edge. He looked like a man who was thoroughly enjoying himself with no plans to hold anything back.

Becca continued to meet him stroke for stroke, her hips bucking off the bed so ferociously, she was shaking her entire queen-size bed frame. No doubt the neighbors above and below could hear her.

"Becca." Her name was strained on his lips as he pulled her closer and sank himself in to the hilt.

"I know," she panted. "I'm close, too." She just hadn't realized how close. Thirty seconds later, she was erupting in a powerful orgasm that had her clinging to Josh's biceps harder than she'd ever clung to anything in her life. Josh followed her over the threshold of ecstasy a few seconds later, throwing his head back in a howl that didn't even sound human.

They both convulsed a few more times before Josh fell to the bed, pulling Becca over on top of him. They lay in complete silence for a few minutes, each straining to catch their breath and comprehend the magnitude of the deed they'd just done.

"Wow," Becca said breaking the silence.

Josh kissed the top of her forehead. "You can say that again."

Chapter 12

That's it... Just a little to the right. Becca held her breath as she attempted to scoot off the bed. She'd spent the past ten minutes trying to strategically move Josh's arm that was draped across her waist and the other that was curled underneath her.

They'd had sex a couple more times throughout the night and each time had been better than the last. Becca had used muscles that had been dormant for years. She wasn't sure she would ever look at her vibrator the same way again.

She successfully moved the arm that was over her waist when she realized one of his legs was over hers. *Great, now what?* She grabbed the side of the bed with her free arm. Maybe the rolling method would work. Anything was worth a try at this point. Josh's six-foot-four-inch frame took up almost her entire queen-size bed. If she wasn't so worried about how she would look when he woke up, she would have stayed nestled in this warm cocoon until the sunlight woke them both up.

At some point in the night they'd turned off the bedroom lights, which meant she could barely see what she was doing in the dark. She built a little momentum and tried to roll out from under his arm and leg, but it didn't work. She froze when Josh stirred slightly.

Once his breathing returned to being steady, Becca tried again. This time she built up enough force to roll right out from under his arm and leg, only to find herself unable to control her stop. She fell flat on her face with a thud that was anything but ladylike. The bed creaked and she heard him groan. She couldn't see Josh, but assumed he'd moved to adjust himself at her sudden departure.

Stifling her own groan at her hard fall, Becca peeked over the side of the bed, eyeing the naked man who had luckily fallen back asleep. She seized the moment and tiptoed out of her bedroom. All the lights were still on in her living room and kitchen. She grabbed her phone and smiled when she noticed her throw and pillows still lying on the floor on her way to the bathroom. *That man surely knows how to work his assets.* It was one asset in particular that had brought her to her knees in more ways than one. Josh's tongue was lethal. In his defense, his kisses should have been fair warning that he knew how to work his mouth to make her surrender. Not that she hadn't surrendered freely… She couldn't be sure if she'd begged or not last night, but she was fairly confident it had been in the equation.

"Oh goodness. I look a mess." Becca stared at her reflection in her bathroom mirror, unable to believe that she'd probably looked like this after the first time they had sex.

She wanted to be back in bed before Josh woke up so that he wouldn't be privy to what she was currently doing. The sun was going to rise soon, so she was short on time. Becca pulled out what she called her magic brush and got to work on her curls. She still wore her high bun to work on occasion, but there was something extremely liberating about letting her hair breathe and her natural curls roam free.

After she'd tamed her hair, she brushed her teeth and applied some lip gloss. "That's too much," she said, puckering her lips. No doubt the lip gloss would be a clear indicator that she'd woken up in the middle of the night to freshen up. She rubbed off the gloss and replaced it with ChapStick.

"Much better." She smacked her lips then stood back and looked at her handiwork. She was still naked and surprisingly enough, although her satin negligee was hanging on the back of her bathroom door, she didn't want to put it on. As liberating as it was to have her hair down, it was just as freeing to roam around naked.

Becca tiptoed back to the bed and placed her phone on her nightstand. She slid back under her sheet, careful not to crush Josh's arm that was still outstretched on her side of the bed. Just when she closed her eyes, her cell phone vibrated. She slowly opened one eye to make sure Josh was still sleeping.

She glanced at her caller ID. *Haley...* Becca answered immediately. "Hey, Haley."

"Hey, Becca. I hope it's not too early."

"Nonsense," Becca whispered. "Is everything okay? Do you have an update on Aunt Penny?"

"Yes. Aunt Penny is holding her own, but they still don't know what's wrong with her. They're going to run more tests today."

"Okay, I'll stop by the hospital later today."

"That would be fine. I'll still be here." Haley grew quiet on the other line.

"Hales, are you okay? Are you crying?"

"Not at the moment," Haley said. "I was actually trying to figure out why you were whispering."

"Oh, I'm not." Becca stole a glance at the still-sleeping Josh. "The sun isn't even up yet, so I'm just groggy from the morning."

"Becca, who are you trying to fool? I've seen you sound more alert after only two hours of sleep."

"I'm not trying to fool you. I'm just tired. I didn't get much sleep. I, um... I was up all night compiling the notes from yesterday's presentation so that I could tell you all about it when you're ready."

Haley was quiet for a few seconds before speaking. "Did Josh leave after he dropped you off last night?"

"Yes."

"Hmm. You answered pretty fast there, bestie."

"That's just because I can't believe you would think he would stay here. We had a good conversation and then he went to his car and left."

"So you let him up to your apartment?"

"Well, yeah, but only for a little while. We had tea. We talked. He's a great listener. Then he kissed me good-night and left."

"You kissed him again?"

Becca hit her forehead. "Well, yes, but no. It was a forehead kiss. Simple. A sign of friendship really."

"I don't know, Becca," Haley said with a laugh.

"Joshua DeLong wasn't looking at you in a friendly way yesterday."

"Oh really?" Becca sat up straighter in the bed. "How was he looking at me?"

"Like a man ready to jump your bones if you so much as smiled at him. Which you did, by the way. You smiled at him in that flirty way that I rarely see you do."

"You think I was flirting with Josh yesterday? You think it was obvious to the other Moguls?"

"Of course it was obvious. And he was staring at you just as hard. It's obvious that he's infatuated with you. When the other men looked at you, he frowned and gave them a look that was anything but friendly. It was a look that said 'back away and back away now.'"

"Humph. I didn't even notice that anyone else was checking me out."

"That's because you were only focused on Joshua DeLong."

"Well, he's a hard man not to focus on." Becca smiled. "He's sexy, funny, hardworking. All around a pretty amazing guy." Just thinking about how much they'd gotten to know each other made her heart feel all warm and tingly.

"Becca?"

"Yes?"

"You had sex with him last night, didn't you?"

"Yes," she said in a dreamy voice.

"I'm so happy for you and I want all the details. But for right now, you better cater to that naked man in your bed who is probably listening to everything we're saying."

Becca's eyes flew to a very awake and very sexy Josh. "Oh my God," Becca said to Haley.

Haley laughed. "You stopped whispering a few minutes ago, so I'm assuming he woke up halfway through
our conversation and I'm assuming right now he's staring at you with those dreamy blue eyes. So I guess we
can chat later when he's not listening."

"Bye, Hales. See you later." Becca placed her phone
back on the nightstand and closed her eyes, refusing to
look at Josh. How embarrassing. It was one thing to tell
your friend about the man you had amazing sex with
right after he left. It was another thing entirely to talk
about him while he was still there.

"How much did you hear?" she asked with her eyes
still closed. Josh grabbed her by the waist and slid her
to him.

"You think I'm sexy." He kissed one side of her
neck. "You think I'm funny." He kissed the other side
of her neck. "You think I'm hardworking." He kissed
one cheek. "And all around, pretty damn amazing." He
kissed her other cheek.

"You added the 'damn' part," she said, finally opening her eyes. When he pulled her in for a kiss, she closed
her eyes again, overcome with the passion this man
could evoke in her.

"And for the record," Josh said as he ran his fingers
over her breasts and down her stomach until he found
the sacred place he was searching for. "You don't have
to get out of bed early to doll yourself up. A little morning breath never hurt anybody and your matted hair
was only a sign of how thoroughly you were sexed last
night. It's flattering really."

Becca's mouth curled into a perfect O. "How did
you… When did you…"

"Becca, you fell out of the bed." His hearty laugh

teased her ears. "It wasn't difficult to figure out what you were doing."

Becca placed her hands over her eyes. "This is so embarrassing. You could have told me that you were up."

"Now, where would the fun have been in that?" Her body immediately jolted when he slipped a finger inside her. "Besides, I've barely slept. I was waiting for you to get enough sleep before we started round four."

"Round four? It hasn't even been twenty-four hours."

"What can I say?" He curled his finger, hitting her sweet spot. She yelped in satisfaction. "I just can't get enough of you, Becca Wright."

She closed her eyes and savored the way his fingers felt moving in and out of her body. *I can't get enough of you, either.* She didn't say it, but she was sure he could tell.

Josh was mesmerized as he watched Becca talk to Aunt Penny. When they'd arrived at the hospital, Becca had told Haley that she would stay with Aunt Penny so that Haley could go home, shower and change. Josh wasn't sure if Becca had expected him to stay too, but he couldn't leave even if she wanted him to.

Since he'd met Becca, she'd constantly been surprising him in ways he hadn't seen coming. Last night had just been the icing on a six-tier cake. Josh had been with his fair share of women, but nothing compared with the night he'd had with Becca. She'd been so responsive in the bedroom and the way they connected sexually had been nothing short of combustible.

It was almost as if their bodies knew each other. He knew how to please her and she knew just what to do to push him to the brink of losing all control. Even now, all he could think about was last night. This morning. The time in the living room. The time in her bedroom. He had work that needed to get done today, but his mind was consumed by Becca.

"Young man, are you just going to stand there and stare at Becca all day, or are you going to come over here and chat with me?"

Josh glanced at Aunt Penny. "I'm sorry, Aunt Penny." He walked over to her hospital bed. "Is there anything that I can get you?"

"Yes, you can tell me what your intentions are with my dear Becca."

"Aunt Penny," Becca exclaimed. "Josh and I are just friends."

Aunt Penny shook her head. "Child, do you think I was born yesterday? That man has been undressing you with his eyes since you both walked into the room."

"He came to check on you, Aunt Penny." Becca glanced from her to Josh and back again. "He's a member of Prescott George. He's the one I was telling you about. The one who's working with the foundation for the gala."

"Oh, honey, this boy is not here to see me." Aunt Penny looked at Josh. "Although I appreciate you visiting me at the hospital, would you please tell my Becca that you're here because you're interested in her?"

Josh shook his head. "I'm here to see you, Aunt Penny." He flashed the woman his million-dollar smile before turning to Becca. "But I'm also here because I'm interested in Becca."

Aunt Penny smiled and patted Becca's hand. "Oh, this one's trouble. Between that face, those eyes and that smile, no wonder you're captivated by him. Guess he's not the ruthless, self-centered, pretty-boy million-aire that Haley said you thought he was, huh, Becca?"

Josh looked at Becca questioningly. "Is that how you described me?"

Becca shrugged. "It was before I knew you. But I also called you charming and persuasive."

Josh laughed. "Well, as long as you got all my assets. And don't forget sexy, funny, hardworking and an all-around amazing guy."

Becca stood up and playfully hit him. "Are we still on that? You shouldn't have been eavesdropping on my conversation."

"You can't whisper." Josh pretended to duck.

"You could have told me that you were awake."

"You could have checked to see if my eyes were open. Guess you were too taken with thoughts about me to glance my way."

As Becca playfully chased Josh around the room, he forgot that Aunt Penny was sitting in the bed until he heard her laughter.

"You're like two peas in a pod."

They both stopped and looked over at Aunt Penny. Becca went back to sit on the bed. "He just likes to rattle my nerves."

"You know what they say," the elderly woman said. "First it starts off with a flirtation and then your feelings grow into something deeper. Then before you know it, you're headed down the aisle."

"That's not going to happen, Aunt Penny." Becca waved her hands in the air. "You know how I feel about marriage. It's not for everyone and it's definitely not for me."

"Me neither," Josh said, shaking his head. "I'm not marriage material. I get bored too easily."

"Me too," Becca agreed. "And I refuse to change myself for a man. If he can't accept me for the woman I am, then he's not worth it. I like stability. Routine."

"I know the feeling." Josh crossed his arms over his chest. "My grandfather used to tell women who inquired about me that just as my work takes me from corporation to corporation, my personal life has a long and varied trajectory."

"My mom thinks that I intentionally push men away to avoid the very thing that I claim I want—stability and routine. I guess I want that, but I also want my freedom. And a little spontaneity every now and then wouldn't hurt."

"See?" Josh said, stretching out his hands. "We both understand each other. We're not unattached because we have to be. We're—"

"Unattached because we choose to be." Becca finished his sentence. Josh high-fived her and when they both turned to Aunt Penny's confused expression, they both laughed.

"Do you hear yourselves?" Aunt Penny asked.

Becca continued to laugh. "Guess you never met two people more imperfect for each other, huh?"

"My dear, you are so wrong." Aunt Penny leaned up and placed her hand on Becca's cheek. "More like I've never met two people more on the same page and in denial about it. Don't you see it?"

Becca and Josh looked at each other, neither responding to Aunt Penny's question. Josh didn't know why Becca wasn't answering, but he knew why he wasn't. After last night, Becca had him questioning everything he thought he knew. Since meeting her, he'd begun thinking about things he never had, and until now, he hadn't given himself the chance to truly think about why he felt so different when he was with Becca or what it meant for them in the long run. All he knew for certain was that when he was with her, it felt right. And when he wasn't, it felt like something was missing. *I wonder if Becca is dealing with the same inner struggle?*

"She is," Aunt Penny said, breaking into his thoughts. He glanced to her, confused.

"She is," Aunt Penny repeated. "The question you're asking yourself in your mind. The answer is 'yes, she is.'"

Josh stared at Aunt Penny, not knowing how to respond. Becca seemed to want to ask more about what they were talking about, but didn't. *How could Aunt Penny know what I'm thinking?* There was just no way.

"I've been around a long time," Aunt Penny said, as if reading his thoughts again. "And when you've seen all that I have, there are some things that you just know. You know I'm right." With that, she closed her eyes, leaving him and Becca to piece together what Aunt Penny had meant.

Josh smiled to Becca as they waited for Aunt Penny to doze off. "She reminds me of my grandfather."

Aunt Penny opened one eye. "Smart man."

"He was. He really would have liked you."

Aunt Penny opened both eyes then and reached for his hand. He walked over to her. "I'm sure I would have liked him too, sweetie. Especially if he was anything like his grandson."

After a few seconds, he released her hand. *Be care-*

ful, Josh, he warned himself as he took a seat in the corner of the hospital room while Aunt Penny dozed off. *A man like you could get used to this.* When Becca caught his eye, he took that voice, bottled it up and stored it in the back of his mind. He didn't know what was going to happen with him and Becca after the gala next month, but for now, he was going to enjoy every moment.

Chapter 13

"Earth to Becca?"

Becca took her feet off her desk, sat up in her seat and motioned for Haley to come into her office.

"Come on in. What's up?"

"We received another donation from someone you met at the movie premiere." Haley took a seat in the chair across from Becca's desk. "That makes the twenty-fifth one to date. And of those, at least half want to donate annually. We still have a way to go, but at this rate, we're on our way to saving the foundation."

Becca clasped her hands together. "That's great news. Everything's working out."

"In more ways than one," Haley said with a sly smile. "You've been out on a date with Josh every night this week."

"Not every night," Becca said. "Two of those nights we just watched Netflix and chilled."

Haley crossed her arms over her chest. "And I know exactly what that means you did, but since you're being difficult, let me rephrase my statement. You've seen Josh every day this week. I'm thinking about setting this man up with an office here since any time we're working late, he's usually here with us."

Becca couldn't contain the big smile that crossed her face. She never would have thought that she and Josh would be seeing so much of one another.

"Where did you go last night?"

"Josh took me to this exclusive rooftop restaurant and we had an entire section to ourselves. After dinner, we went to the downstairs club and danced all night."

Haley's hands flew up. "Wait, you danced? Leanna and I tried to get you to go dancing a couple months ago and you turned us down claiming you're a bad dancer."

"Hales, you know I'm a bad dancer."

"Of course I know that. The point is, you're a bad dancer, but you danced with Josh?"

"I know. I can barely believe it myself. Guaranteed, he spent most of the night secretly laughing at my hideous moves. You know, men who I've dated in the past have asked me to refrain from dancing in public because of how bad I am. But Josh couldn't care less. In fact, he even made a fool of himself too just so that I wouldn't feel alone."

She thought about some of the outrageous things he'd done to take the spotlight off her. He was amazing. He was more than amazing.

A noise in the hallway got Becca's and Haley's attention.

"Come on in, Stacy," Becca called when she saw the tip of her shoe in the doorway.

"Sorry," the teen said, stepping into the room. "I was just bringing you this." Stacy handed Becca a stack of new student profiles she'd entered into the intranet.

"Thank you," Becca said. "You've been doing great these past couple weeks. Haley and I are really proud of you."

"Thanks," Stacy said with a big smile before she went back to the reception desk.

"Unbelievable," Haley said when she was out of earshot. "We couldn't get Stacy to work hard enough when she first got here. Then you start dating Joshua DeLong and suddenly she's giving us her A game—as long as you keep her updated on your dates and don't call her out for eavesdropping."

Becca laughed. "He certainly has the ability to captivate women no matter what age they are. You should have seen how Aunt Penny was eating out of the palm of his hand."

"I hate that I missed it." Haley snapped her fingers. "Where is your boyfriend taking you tonight?"

"He's not my boyfriend." Becca played with the pen on her desk. "We've just been going out on a few dates. That's all."

"Whatever you say." Haley didn't look convinced. "So where is he taking you?"

"Usually his mother has him and his brothers over for dinner on Sunday, so he invited me to join him before we head someplace that he refuses to tell me about. He just mentioned that I should wear a nice dress."

"Hold on! You're meeting his mom tonight?"

"Yeah." Becca looked at the clock on her wall. "He's picking me up from my place in two hours."

"Then why are you still here?" Haley asked. "Meeting his mom is a big deal. I never would have asked you to work today had I known. Work can wait until tomorrow."

"It's no big deal," Becca said, brushing her off. "He mentioned that his mom was impressed by the foundation when he told her about it. I'm sure she just wants to chat with me."

"Oh, Becca." Haley shook her head. "Has it been that long since you've met parents of a man you're dating? Josh wouldn't ask you to meet his mom if it wasn't getting serious between you two."

"Haley, you're going to freak me out. I really don't think it's that big of a deal."

"Yes, it is," Stacy said, peeking her head into Becca's office. "For what it's worth, I agree with Haley. You should go home and prepare to meet your future mother-in-law."

"Guys, you're nuts." Becca laughed nervously. "True, Josh and I have gotten closer over the past couple weeks, but it isn't that serious. We talk about his family a lot, so it's perfectly normal for him to want me to meet his mother."

Two hours later, Becca's stomach was in a ball of knots. *This isn't normal. This isn't normal at all. Why did I agree to this?*

"Are you okay?" Josh asked.

Becca stopped fidgeting in the passenger seat. "Of course. Why wouldn't I be?"

"Just a wild guess, but I assumed you were nervous about meeting my mom and brothers."

"Me? No way." She tossed her hand in the air and shook her head. "I'm meeting your mom and brothers.

No big deal, right? Nothing too serious. You want me to meet them because we're always talking about them. It's completely natural for us to meet. Right? Friends get introduced to parents all the time and we're friends, right?" *Stop rambling!*

"Right," Josh said with a laugh.

"Right to which part?"

"All of it. It's no big deal. It's natural for you to meet them. And we are friends."

"Right."

Josh looked at her. "Right."

Five minutes later, they pulled into the driveway of his mom's home in a predominantly African American lower-middle-class neighborhood. Becca had been to the neighborhood before. A lot of her students were from there.

"You look amazing," Josh said as he helped her out of his French blue Bugatti.

"Thank you." She'd chosen to wear a deep green strapless dress that hugged her figure in the same way that the dress she wore for the movie premiere did. When she'd picked out the dress during her shopping trip with Haley, the associate had told her that this particular green really made her light brown eyes pop. Josh was staring intently into them, so she mentally high-fived the associate.

She wouldn't have thought it was possible, but Josh looked even more handsome than he normally did. Tonight he was wearing a sleek black brocade jacket, matching black slacks and a light gray shirt underneath. Black-and-gray Stacy Adams shoes topped off his classic ensemble.

"Don't be nervous," he said, leading her up the porch stairs.

Easier said than done.

Josh waved at a few neighbors who called out his name before pulling out his keys and opening the front door. It was so quiet when they entered, Becca thought no one was home.

"Is anyone here?" she asked him.

"They're here. You'll see soon." Within seconds of him making the statement, cheers and hollers erupted from down the hall.

"Come on, I'll introduce you to the rest of my brothers."

Becca nodded, but internally she was still trying to calm her nerves. They rounded the corner to the living room where three men just as tall as Josh were standing in front of a large television that almost took up an entire wall.

"Fellas, we made it." At the sound of Josh's voice, each man turned to face them. *Oh my.* Becca felt frozen in place as she stared into the faces of men who were almost as attractive as Josh. In her personal opinion, Josh was a lot sexier, but his brothers were definitely the type of men that would stop women in their tracks. She was proof.

"Becca, I'd like for you to meet Sebastian and Ryan, and you've already met Logan."

"Well, hello again," Logan said, coming up to hug her.

"Hey, Logan." Becca returned his hug. "Did you ever figure out the name of that woman you were with?"

"Yeah." Logan sheepishly rubbed the back of his head. "It was Rita."

"Rita?" Becca laughed. "You weren't even close. By the time we left, you hadn't even made it to the *R*'s yet."

"She didn't let me. When I hit the *M*'s, she took pity and decided that I was more skillful in other extracurricular activities." Logan raised both his eyebrows.

"I'm sure she did," Becca said with a laugh. She turned to his other brothers. "Nice to meet you both."

"It's nice to meet the woman who has my brother's nose wide-open," Sebastian said, pulling her in for a hug. Josh cleared his throat, but Sebastian shrugged it off. Ryan hugged her next.

Becca glanced at the television. "We didn't mean to interrupt the baseball game."

"Don't worry about it," Ryan said. "Meeting you is much more interesting. You look beautiful." Ryan gave her an appreciative glance.

"Keep your eyes in your head." Becca looked over her shoulder when Josh spoke. The protectiveness she heard in his voice was undeniable.

"You better listen to him, Ryan," Logan said. "I kissed the back of Becca's hand and Josh was ready to punch me for getting too close to his woman."

Becca waited for Josh to deny what Logan was saying, but he stayed quiet. Josh's brothers exchanged a knowing look. Becca seemed to be the only one out of the loop.

"Is that my oldest son who just walked through the door?"

All five of them turned at the sound of Josh's mom in the living room doorway. Becca glanced from Josh to his mom. They looked so much alike, she had to do a double take.

"Hi, Mom." Josh hugged her, but his mother's eyes stayed on Becca.

"Hi, son. Is this Becca?"

"Hi, Mrs. DeLong. It's very nice to meet you."

"Oh, please, dear, call me Cindy." Cindy pulled Becca in for a hug. "I've been waiting to meet you for weeks."

"You have?"

"Of course I have. For the past two Sundays my son has been grinning from ear to ear. I knew it had to be a woman, so we cajoled the information out of him." Cindy glanced from her to Josh. "And he was right about your beauty."

Becca's face flushed. "Thank you so much, Cindy. He was right about yours, too."

"Aren't you the sweetest. Now, I hope my son hasn't been working you too hard for the gala. He tends to take his position at Prescott George very seriously."

"Oh no, ma'am. Josh has been great. The Aunt Penny Foundation has been receiving numerous donations ever since we started working together. You raised an amazingly talented son." Becca stole a glance at Josh only to find him already staring at her intently. He'd been doing that a lot lately. Most of the time, she could feel his eyes on her. Other times—like now—his penetrating stare caught her off guard. *How am I supposed to think straight when he looks at me like that?* She was so wrapped up in his eyes she forgot that they had an audience.

Becca turned back to Cindy. "I know you've probably already been cooking most of the day, but is there anything I can help you with?"

Cindy looked down at Becca's dress. "Sweetie, you aren't exactly dressed for cooking in the kitchen."

"That's your son's fault," Becca said with a laugh. "He told me to dress nice, but he won't tell me where we're going after dinner. But I don't mind helping out in this dress. Especially if you need help." To further prove her point, Becca pulled her hair tie out of her clutch and pulled her curls up into a high ponytail.

Cindy looked at her sons, then Josh. "Oh, she's a keeper." Cindy tapped Becca's arms. "Well, first let me give you a tour of the house since my son forgot his manners."

"Sorry, Mom," Josh yelled after them.

Becca followed Cindy through the immaculate house, then stepped into the dining room. Once there, Cindy set the table and Becca helped her.

"So, let's chat. You have to excuse my excitement, but I'm surrounded by men most of the time."

Becca smiled. "No worries. I think your sons wanted me to get out of their hair anyway so that they could finish watching the game."

"I know at least one of my sons didn't want to let you out of his sight."

"We've been together a lot lately, so he probably wants to watch the game, too." As soon as the comment left her mouth, she realized she'd said too much. Cindy was looking at her with a knowing look similar to the one Aunt Penny had worn when they'd visited her in the hospital.

Becca followed Cindy to the kitchen. Once they were there, Cindy gave Becca all the ingredients to toss a salad while she finished making the macaroni and cheese.

"Has Josh told you anything about his father?"

Becca looked up from the salad. "Yes. He mentioned what an amazing and hardworking man he was."

"He was." Cindy smiled. "He was one of the hardest-working men I've ever known. There's not a day that goes by that I don't miss that man. Sometimes—when the house is quiet and the boys aren't here visiting—I can hear my husband's voice drift through the house as if he never left. I know it might sound crazy, but I almost feel like he's here with me sometimes."

"That's understandable," Becca said. "He was your husband. The father of your children. You loved him. It's natural that it would seem as if he still exists somehow."

Becca tried not to get nervous since she could feel Cindy observing her. "Becca, he was more than my husband and the father of my children. He was my one true love and the man who I vowed in front of family, friends and God to love and honor with all my heart. Have you ever been in love before?"

Becca shook her head. "No, ma'am. I thought I was, but what I had wasn't true love."

They were silent for a couple minutes before Cindy started talking again. "You know, when my husband and I moved into this house, we didn't even have enough money to pinch together to buy food. We didn't mind at the time. We were just happy to own our own home. Then one day I found out I was pregnant. When we had Josh, we knew we couldn't live off scraps, and although my husband was doing well as a mechanic, we needed more to raise a baby.

"So there were times when we had to steal food to

make sure we didn't starve. We weren't proud of those times and I know that my husband hated to stoop to stealing, but we did what we had to do to survive."

Becca let Cindy's words marinate in her mind before responding. "Sometimes I think it's harder to make a difficult decision and execute that choice than it is to do the right thing, because the right thing is not always necessarily right for you."

"That's true." Cindy put the macaroni in the oven and went to stir the lemonade. "My husband didn't marry me to stand by his side for the easy decisions. He married me so that he could have a partner to stand by him for the difficult decisions. A partner who wouldn't pass judgment and would appreciate the value of a dollar. Let me ask you something, Becca. How much does a loaf of bread cost?"

Becca thought about it. "I'm not sure. It's been a long time since I've been to the grocery store."

"Have you been to a Laundromat recently? Do you know how much that costs?"

Becca shook her head. *I wonder why she's asking me all these questions.* "No, ma'am. I haven't been to a Laundromat recently."

"That's okay," Cindy said. "Because after this conversation, I'm sure you'll look it up." They worked in silence a bit more until it dawned on Becca why Cindy was asking. And the more she thought about the reasoning, the more annoyed she got.

"Cindy, I may not know how much a loaf of bread or washing a load of laundry costs, but I do know how much it costs to buy a stamp, because I buy stamps all the time to send letters to universities and colleges on behalf of my students. I also know how much a notebook and pencils cost. All school supplies really, because I'm always buying them for the kids in our program."

Becca tossed the salad. "If the purpose of your questions are to try to see if I live beyond my means or if I understand the value of a dollar, then I can assure you that I know the meaning of hard work."

"Josh doesn't know how much a loaf of bread costs and he doesn't do his own laundry."

Huh? What is she trying to say? Becca had been prepared to meet the sweet woman Josh had described to her, so she had to admit she was a little surprised by Cindy's behavior.

"Josh also knows the value of a dollar," Becca said. "Not knowing how much bread costs and not doing his own laundry doesn't change the fact that you can tell he's a man who has worked hard for what he has, and although he may allow himself to enjoy luxury every now and then, he appreciates every dollar he's made."

Cindy smiled. "My son can't be with a weak-minded woman, Becca. He needs a woman who will put up a fight on his behalf. A woman who will stand her ground no matter what. A woman who will be there for the hard times and celebrate the good. Josh has always been my assertive child. My argumentative child. The son who always strove to be the best man he could to uphold his father's memory…his legacy. Josh has worked very hard to get where he is today and when all is said and done, the woman he chooses to spend the rest of his life with cannot be a pushover."

Becca observed Cindy, hoping that she had more to say. *Is she insulting me or complimenting me?* She wasn't sure. When Cindy didn't say anything more, Becca stopped messing with the salad. "Cindy, is there a reason you're telling me all this? Josh and I are just friends, but I feel like you know something that I don't. Or you have more to say, but won't come out and say it."

"He also needs a woman who won't settle." Cindy winked. "And there's nothing I know that you and Josh don't already know."

Oh my gosh, she's talking in riddles. Becca laughed to herself. In some ways, Josh reminded her so much of his mom.

"You know, Becca, Josh has never brought a woman home to meet me before."

Becca had begun washing the utensils but now she stopped and turned to Cindy. "As an adult? Or never as in never ever?"

"Never as in never ever," Cindy said with a laugh. "So it's only fair that you know you passed all my tests with flying colors."

"Was that why you were asking me all those questions? You were testing me?"

"Sure was." Cindy walked over to Becca. "I knew the minute I looked at you that you were an amazing woman. If I'm being honest, I also have to admit that I've already looked up all the work you've done with the foundation. Josh is infatuated with you. Anyone can see it if they're in the same room with you two. But as much as I love my son, he can't have a woman who's a pushover. He needs a woman who will stick up for him even if—"

"Even if it's against someone who claims to care about him," Becca said, nodding her head.

"Exactly, because in his line of work, someone

will always be hoping that he fails and certain people who claim to have his best interest at heart, won't. Sometimes the same people who motivate you and drive your determination are the same people who could contribute to your failure—if you give them that power. Some of those people may even be your family. Your own blood."

Becca thought about his brothers and mom. Even though she'd only been around them for a short time, it was obvious they cared deeply about one another. *I can't imagine any of them trying to screw him over.* She didn't want to interrupt Cindy to ask her to clarify, so she left it alone.

"Now, my son isn't a saint and he's good at what he does, but he needs a good woman who will have his back no matter what. And, sweetie, I was already impressed by you before we met. Seeing you today only confirms my assumption."

Becca was sure Cindy could tell she was hanging on every word. "And what might that assumption be?"

Cindy lightly touched Becca's cheek before going back to cooking. "I'm sure my assumption is something that's already floating around in that pretty little head of yours, so you'll figure it out. Now, enough with the fun and games. Let's finish this meal so that my sons can eat. How good are you in the kitchen?"

Becca looked at all the food and ingredients still left on the kitchen counter. "Um, any chance you have a recipe book I can follow?"

Cindy laughed. "Oh, Becca. We'll make a wife out of you yet."

Becca's eyes grew large.

"I'm kidding." Cindy laughed. "Just some future-mother-in-law humor."

Becca swallowed and suddenly wished she was near a fan.

"Oh, dear, you and my son are perfect for each other."

Chapter 14

Josh glanced over at Becca as the rich tunes of the Miami Symphony Orchestra filled the Arsht Center. She was completely enthralled with the performance. Josh didn't think she'd so much as blinked since they'd arrived.

When he'd heard her briefly talk about how much she missed playing the violin and had seen the look of longing in her eyes, he'd known in that moment that he wanted to take her some place that might help her get that spark back.

Becca was so acutely focused on the performance that all Josh could do was watch her in complete awe. He'd gotten the best box seats he could find, wanting her to have the best view possible. Her features were relaxed as she listened to the soloists move from one piece to the next flawlessly.

Josh sat a little straighter in his seat as he tried to concentrate on the piece that was currently being performed. His mind wandered to dinner at his mom's place earlier. Everything had gone better than expected and by the time his mom and Becca had finished preparing dinner, they had been like two peas in a pod. Even his brothers had commented on the fact that they hadn't seen their mom smile quite like that in so long.

He wasn't surprised that by the end of the dinner, Becca had his entire family eating out of the palm of her hand. She may claim that her social capabilities fell short of her other attributes, but Josh had to disagree. Seeing Becca with his family was simple. Easy. She fit in so perfectly that Josh had spent most of the night just watching them all interact, amazed that this woman had brought a brilliant light to his life that he hadn't even known was missing. She was remarkable. Truly and utterly remarkable.

"That was amazing," Becca said, turning to him before standing.

"Huh? What?" It took a few seconds for him to register that everyone was giving the musicians a standing ovation. Josh immediately stood to join in on the excitement.

After the performance, they stepped outside into the warm July night. Becca was still on cloud nine. "Thank you so much for taking me. That was amazing. The entire night was amazing really."

Josh smiled. "I'm glad you enjoyed yourself. It was nice seeing you so captivated by the performance."

"I was beyond captivated." She clasped her hands together. "It was truly outstanding. Fantastic. Magnificent."

He laughed when she did a three-hundred-and-sixty-degree turn on the sidewalk. "Glad to hear it." He glanced down the street at a jazz lounge he'd been to a few times. "Are you up for a little jazz? Or do you want to call it a night since we have work in the morning?"

"I'm game to continue the night if you are."

"Great." He took her hand in his and began walking the short distance to the lounge. Her eyes were focused on their enclosed hands and more than anything, he wished he knew what she was thinking. Unable to resist, he asked.

"What's going on in that beautiful head of yours?"

Becca looked up from their clasped hands. "Nothing." Her mouth may have been saying it was nothing, but her eyes were saying something else entirely.

"Doesn't seem like nothing." Josh stopped walking and rubbed the side of her cheek. "Sure you don't want to talk it out?" Her eyes dropped to his lips and he felt that same kick in his gut he felt every time she looked at him like that.

"I was thinking about the fact that I've never made it past the first level of your yacht. I'd love to see more of it sometime."

"I'd love to give you a personal tour whenever you're ready. Maybe if you didn't look so sexy, we'd make it off the top level before the sun came up and we had to go to work."

Becca giggled. "I love my condo, but yes, I was thinking we need a change of scenery." Her hand rose to rub at her earlobe.

And that's when he knew. "That's not what you were thinking. You may want to see more of my yacht, but that's not what you were just thinking about."

She knit her brows. "How can you be so sure?"

"Because you just rubbed your earlobe. You always rub your earlobe when you're lying."

"I do not." She playfully hit his arm. "I was playing with my earring. I really do want to see the rest of your yacht."

"Tell you what." He placed his hands around her waist and pulled her closer to him. "I'm overdue for a few days off. I was planning on taking a mini vacation after the gala next month, but why don't we both get away for a little while? Could you spare a few days away from the foundation?"

"I'm sure I could, but where would we go?"

Josh smiled slyly. "Leave that up to me."

"I don't get any hints? How will I know what to pack?"

"Hmm, I guess you're right. Well, all I'll say is that it's on an island."

Becca grinned. "Sounds like my kind of vacation. Although I'd enjoy going anywhere with you." Her face grew serious. Josh assumed she'd said more than she wanted to say.

He leaned his forehead against hers. "It doesn't matter what we're doing. I always enjoy being with you, too." Her body relaxed at his words.

As it was most of the time he was with Becca, he didn't hear the voice calling his name until it was a couple feet away. Josh lifted his forehead from Becca's and saw fellow Prescott George member Daniel Cobb standing outside of the jazz lounge.

Josh waved as Daniel walked over with Angela, his fiancée.

Josh remembered meeting Angela for the first time

at a Moguls event. He'd known the minute he met her that Daniel was a goner. It had been in the way they'd interacted with each other. The way they'd flirted with one another when they thought no one was paying attention. He was glad to see that Daniel had come to his senses and proposed. They were perfect for one another.

Josh couldn't help but turn to Becca and wonder if they would end up as happy as Daniel and Angela.

"Hey, Daniel." The men dabbed fists before Josh turned to hug Angela. "Angela, it's good seeing you again."

"You too," Angela said, returning his hug.

"Daniel, I don't think I had a chance to introduce you at our last meeting, but this is Becca Wright, director of public relations for The Aunt Penny Foundation. Becca, this is Daniel Cobb, and this beauty on his arm is Angela Trainor."

"Nice to meet you." Becca shook their hands. Daniel and Angela returned the sentiments. All four of them walked into the lounge and got a seat together in a booth in the corner. The jazz session was in between sets, so the place was pretty quiet.

"Were you both at the Arsht Center, as well?" Josh asked.

"Yes, we were," Daniel said. "I assisted one of the soloists in purchasing his latest home a couple months ago and he invited me to tonight's performance. I'm actually glad we ran into you both. Josh, I've been meaning to catch up with you."

"Me too, man, but we've both been busy."

Both Josh and Daniel looked at Becca and Angela.

"It's fine." Angela waved her hand. "Why don't you

two go to the bar to chat, and Becca and I will stay here and get to know one another."

Josh looked from Angela to Becca. "Would you mind?"

"Not at all," Becca said with a smile. "I'll still be here when you're finished." On instinct, he leaned down and kissed her before getting out of the booth. Had they not had an audience, Josh may have gotten carried away with the kiss.

Once they were at the bar and had ordered Scotch on the rocks, Josh finally noticed that Daniel was wearing this silly grin on his face.

"What's that look for?"

"I'm not sure I believe what I see," Daniel said, glancing back at the women. "Bad-boy rebel Joshua DeLong who was voted Most Likely to Never Marry by the Moguls is completely head over heels for a woman? I never thought I'd see the day."

Josh grinned. "Man, she completely took me by surprise. We haven't even talked about what all of this means."

"Wait a minute. You were the one who told me that men need to be up front with women regarding their intentions when I was all up in arms about Angela. Not taking your own advice, DeLong?"

"I know, man, I know. We're heading out of town for a few days and I'm hoping to have a conversation with her soon."

"Well, don't take too long," Daniel said. "I was impressed by Becca's presentation at the meeting and I know a lot of Moguls felt the same way I did. I'm sure you didn't miss all the eyes that were on her. You don't want to wait too long to tell her how you feel."

Josh took a swig of his Scotch. "What if I'm still trying to figure that out? I mean, I'm pretty sure I know how I feel. Or how I could feel. But telling her... I don't know, man. We were both pretty clear about our views on relationships."

"Look, I don't know how your talks have gone, but take it from a man who spent weeks in denial—you and Becca are already in a relationship. Whether you label it or not, that's what it is. And from the possessive glances you keep shooting her way—the same possessive stares you were giving her at the PG meeting—I'm sure that you already know where this is headed. Everything else is just protocol."

Daniel looked at Angela. "And trust me, once you accept the fact that this woman has stolen your heart and will never return it back to you, you can focus on building your future together. Being a bachelor is overrated and now that I'm engaged to Angela, I can't imagine how I ever got through life without her."

Josh looked at Becca again, who was laughing at something Angela had said. "I know the feeling."

"Okay, now that we've settled that, let's get down to business." Daniel's voice grew serious. "Regarding Ashton. We have several key members on board with dethroning him from his presidency, but as I've stated before, this won't be easy. With Ashton getting wind of our plan and being on the defense, it's now more important than ever that our strategy is foolproof."

"I agree." Josh took another swig of his Scotch. "I was able to recruit several more members, as well. I think a few others may join our movement, but right now, they're still afraid of going against a Rollins. A meeting with all the members on board with our strategy will strengthen our united force and prove to those stragglers that now is the time for them to pick a side—that when all the Rollins cards fall, they'll want to be on the right side. Our side."

"That sounds good. Let's set up the meeting."

"I'll get on it tomorrow. You reach out to any members whose support we have who have been talking to you directly. I have a feeling in my gut that Prescott George will be turning over a new leaf very soon, and my gut never steers me wrong."

Josh tried his best to stay focused as Daniel continued discussing business. On their own accord, his eyes made their way to Becca's once more. She smiled when she caught him staring. *Yeah, I'm in trouble.*

"You have it so bad."

Becca turned to Angela. "Hmm, what?"

"You already know what I'm talking about. We may have just met, but take it from a woman who fell in love with a Mogul. Once you start falling, you might as well face the inevitable because there is no way that you can reverse the process."

Becca laughed. "Am I that obvious?"

"It's not just you, Becca. I actually think Josh is even more obvious. I haven't known him for that long, but I can tell he's really taken with you. I think it's adorable."

Becca leaned her head back in the booth. "I feel like I'm in way over my head. Like I'm not even the same person I was a month ago. I used to be so focused on work and ensuring that the foundation is successful. Now I feel like Josh has hijacked most of my thoughts. It's like my entire world is consumed by him right now."

Angela placed a hand on her arm. "I know that it

must feel like falling for a man like him is somehow taking over your identity, but that's just what happens when two people are in love."

"We're not in love." Becca answered a little too quickly. Judging by the skeptical look Angela was giving her, she didn't believe her.

"Whether you're in love, headed in that direction or still feeling each other out, my point is that you are still the same person you were before you met Josh. Tell me this—when you're together, does he ask you to be anyone but yourself?"

Becca reflected back to the time when he made himself look crazy dancing just so that she wouldn't feel awkward. "No, he always allows me to be myself."

"Does he ever seem to want to take away from the things you feel are important in life?"

She thought about Josh's devotion to the foundation. "No, he never seems that way."

"And lastly, does he include you in important aspects of his life, or does he keep his worlds separate?"

Becca reflected on the time they spent in the animal shelter and earlier today when they had spent time with his family. "He includes me."

"Then, hon, you can't look at it as if you are losing yourself in the process of falling for a man like Josh. Think of it as gaining an ally. A partner. Someone who understands you in ways no one else does. Being together is making your lives better, more complete. Not the opposite."

Becca let Angela's words sink in as her gaze found Josh's for the fifth time in the past thirty minutes. She was right. Becca had to focus on the positive and not allow past experience to impact her and Josh's relationship.

"You're a smart woman," Becca said, sipping the martini she'd ordered. "You've managed to put everything in perspective."

"I only said what you had already figured out but didn't want to acknowledge. Plus, I just went through this with Daniel. I didn't want to admit my feelings for him and in our case he was my boss at the time, so I was really going through an inner struggle." Angela looked at Daniel from across the lounge. "Now when I look at that man over there I can't imagine what my life would be like without him in it."

Becca smiled as she watched Angela and Daniel look at one another, love prevalent in both their gazes. It was so easy to imagine her and Josh hanging out with the happy couple way past the gala celebration. But first, she needed to talk to Josh and figure out where his head was at. She had a feeling their mini vacation would be the perfect time to do so.

Chapter 15

"Oh my gosh, Allison. I can't believe you told Mom about my trip."

Allison rolled her eyes. "Oh, come on, Becca, you're being a drama queen. Had I known that it was a secret, I never would have said anything."

"Hello! Earth to Allison." Becca flailed her arms. "Have you met our mother? The woman who has made me go on several blind dates and donated thousands of dollars to date auctions on my behalf? The woman who wants me to get married so bad that she once went to a psychic to make sure that I hadn't secretly decided to become a nun in hopes of never having to say 'I do'? Have you met that woman?"

Allison stopped walking down the crowded block in downtown Miami and glared at Becca. "Listen, Becca, I said I'm sorry. I was really excited when you called and asked me to go shopping with you. It just so happened that I was at our parents' house for breakfast. You can reprimand me all you want *after* your vacation, but for right now, we have to go purchase a few necessary items for your trip."

Becca rolled her eyes and continued to follow Allison down the block. *Next time, I'm calling Haley or Leanna.* She didn't say the words out loud because she didn't want to hurt her sister's feelings, but she made a mental note to always text her sister first to ask if she was with their mother *before* spilling any details about a man.

Becca hadn't hung out with her sister in months and figured a quick shopping trip would be good for them. She was meeting Josh on his yacht tomorrow morning then leaving for their three-day mini vacation.

Growing up, she and Allison had been extremely close. But then Allison got married, had kids, started her catering business, while Becca was still just... Becca. She'd dived fully into work and after breaking her engagement with Rich, their conversations about men, dating and the possibility of a family in the future dwindled.

"Here we are," Allison said, stopping in front of a lingerie store. "It's supposed to be one of the hottest new boutiques in town, but I haven't checked it out yet. Come on." Allison pulled her inside.

"Welcome to Bare Sophistication," a salesclerk said as soon as they entered the door.

"Let's start over here." Becca followed Allison to a table with folded lace panties and matching bra sets. "What type of lingerie are you looking for?"

"Well, we'll be gone for three days, but I need more

than three days' worth. Josh has been over to my place a lot, so he's seen almost everything I have."

"Oh, has he now?" Allison raised an eyebrow. "My, my… We definitely have so much to catch up on, sis. Especially since Joshua DeLong managed to clear those cobwebs from your lady parts."

"Actually, I'm sure Sherry who works at Leanna's salon did that."

"Huh?"

Becca shook her head. "Never mind. Let's just look for about five or six sets. And maybe a teddy or sexy camisole, too."

"Who are you and what have you done with my sister?"

Becca laughed. "It's all Josh's fault. The man has the stamina of a speedster on steroids and because of him, my sex drive is at an all-time high."

Allison nodded her finger at Becca. "Oh, I like him. I like him a lot."

Twenty minutes later, the store had practically emptied and Becca had only found a couple pieces she liked, but hadn't tried them on yet.

"Becca, what about this?" Allison lifted a lilac teddy in the air.

"No. It's not what I'm looking for."

Allison shook her head. "You're being so picky. Unless you try some stuff on, you'll never know what looks good on your figure. You have amazing curves, yet you're holding pieces that won't complement them. You're finally back to sharing your curves with the world. Don't hide them from the important man in your life."

Her sister was right. She was being picky for no reason.

"Can I help you with anything?"

Allison and Becca turned to a beautiful woman with long wavy brown hair and big round eyes. Becca was about to say they were fine, but Allison spoke first.

"Actually, my little sis is trying to find lingerie that will make her millionaire boyfriend weak in the knees. Can you suggest some knock-you-on-your-butt pieces, because we've been here for over twenty minutes and she isn't liking anything I choose."

"Allison!" Becca squealed.

The woman laughed. "No worries. I have two older sisters so I know how you feel. My name is Summer and I own the boutique, so I know it inside and out."

"Nice to meet you, Summer." Becca extended her hand. "My name is Becca and this loudmouth over here is my sister, Allison."

"Nice to meet you both." Summer glanced at the items in her hand. "Are you just trying to make him salivate or are you also shopping for a special occasion?"

"A little of both," Allison said on Becca's behalf. "She's going to an island for three days with one of the sexiest men in Miami and she needs to have enough lingerie for her trip and for when she gets back."

"Ah, the millionaire boyfriend," Summer said. "I see."

Becca glared at Allison before turning back to Summer. "He's not my boyfriend, but my sister's right. I want to knock him off his feet."

"Tell you what. How about I put these items you already chose in a fitting room so you can try them on.

While you're in there, I'll pick out some more pieces. Sound good?"

"That would be great," Becca said, relieved. "Clearly I need help."

Summer laughed. "That's what I'm here for. I promise you, Becca. By the time I'm finished with you, you'll have an entirely new sexy lingerie wardrobe. And when you go on your fabulous trip, your millionaire man won't know what hit him."

Becca smiled. "That's precisely what I'm hoping for."

Josh had just made it to the Southern Royal Yacht Club gate when Becca was getting out of the car he'd sent to pick her up from her place. As usual, her beauty kicked him right in the gut.

He lifted his Ray-Bans and extended a hand to help her out of the car. "Hey, beautiful."

"Hey yourself, handsome."

Unable to help himself, he pulled her in for a kiss. Her lips melted into his and by the time he reluctantly pulled away the driver had already taken her bags out of the car.

"I'll take your bags," Josh said after he tipped the driver. Becca followed him up the ramp to his yacht.

"I'm impressed."

He glanced at her. "By what?"

"The silver Porsche Panamera you sent to pick me up. It's not every day a girl gets picked up in a luxury car as opposed to the standard vehicle."

"Well, it's not every day a man is trying to impress a luxury car enthusiast such as yourself. You make me step up my game." *In more ways than one...*

When they boarded his yacht, Josh got a little nervous, a feeling that had otherwise been foreign to him—until he met Becca. This was the first time he would be giving her a full tour of the yacht and since they'd be spending a lot of time on it for the next few days, he wanted her to like it.

"Can you wait here while I put your bags away?"

"Sure."

He took her bags to one of the two master cabins and returned. "Okay, let's start with the third floor and make our way down." Josh started with the Captain's quarters, the top deck and Jacuzzi, and the lounge. He introduced Becca to the crew, including the interior staff, the deckhands and the chef who would all be accompanying them on their trip.

"I never thought about you having an actual yacht staff," Becca said as he led her to the second level.

"When I'm docked in South Beach, I don't have a staff on board. But when I actually go places on my yacht, I definitely need my crew for a vessel this size."

"I don't even know where we're going, but I'm getting even more excited now."

Josh grinned. "Good. Hopefully this next section will take you to an even higher level of excitement. It's one of my favorite parts of the yacht." They walked through a couple sliding doors.

"Oh my goodness…" Had Josh not been standing so close to Becca, he wouldn't have heard her soft words.

"This is what I call my entertainment haven." Floor-to-ceiling glass covered the entire room, which was adorned with mahogany trimmings. Crisp white furniture sat in the center of the room surrounding a circular glass table.

Josh walked Becca over to another set of sliding

doors that led to a small yet functional gym. On the opposite side sat doors leading to the middle deck, where a lavish indoor plunge pool served as the center attraction.

"The pool is made of a natural stone you can only get in Spain. Took me years to find the perfect stone."

"It's breathtaking." Becca ran her fingers over the stone pool. "I've never seen more elegant decor."

"Thank you." His heart swelled. "Your opinion means a lot to me. I went through four yacht interior designers to pull off this look, but it was worth it to get this end result. If you follow me, I'll show you the bedrooms."

They walked back through the all-glass lounge to the other side of the yacht. There were four rooms on this side of the vessel, each with the same elegant design. "When designing the bedrooms, I made sure that the mahogany-and-white theme was present throughout. Each is equipped with a whirlpool tub and standing shower. The glass accent pieces bring in the finished look. Not exactly kid friendly, but the only people who really ever stay here are my brothers and typically they're bringing women back with them who appreciate the style."

Becca walked into one of his favorite rooms, which had a circular mirror behind the bed. It was tastefully done, but he had to admit, he'd love to get Becca in front of that mirror.

"Logan loves this bedroom."

"Has he brought Rita here yet?"

"No," Josh said with a laugh. "My brothers are really particular about the type of women they bring here. Usually it's women they're trying to pursue who are giving them a run for their money. And even then, those women have to go through my screening process."

"Your screening process?" Becca laughed. "It makes sense given you're a Mogul and a millionaire. I just never expected you to implement something like that."

"This yacht is my baby. I don't let just anyone on Soul's First Kiss."

"I meant to ask you… Why did you name your yacht Soul's First Kiss?"

Josh curled his lips to the side. "Maybe I'll tell you one day."

"Oh, so it's like that?" She playfully hit his bicep.

"You have to go through a screening too, Ms. Wright."

"Seriously? Haven't I already passed the screening?"

"That depends."

"On what?"

Josh tried to think of something. "That depends on if you finally finish that kiss we started when the car dropped you off or if you're going to make me show you the indoor theater, kitchen, dining room, the rest of the lower main deck and the two master bedrooms."

Becca gasped. "Oh my gosh. No wonder you can't imagine yourself living anywhere else."

Josh laughed at her complete disregard for his ultimatum. "Does that mean I don't get my kiss?"

Becca smiled cunningly. "If you tell me where we're going, I'll kiss you."

"Oh really?"

"Yes really."

Although he knew she would probably kiss him anyway, he actually wanted to tell her their destination.

"We're going to an island called Purity Haven."

Her eyes filled with excitement. "I've never heard of it before, but it sounds divine."

"It's a small island in the Bahamas. I asked my captain to take the scenic route, so we'll be there in a few hours."

Becca sported the most beautiful smile that he'd ever seen. It was so contagious, it made him smile. He watched her sashay in his direction, her eyes dropping from his to his lips.

"Thank you for suggesting we take this much-needed break from reality."

He wrapped his arms around her at the same time hers encircled his neck. "You're very welcome. Thank you for agreeing to join me on this adventure."

Becca didn't respond, but instead glanced around the bedroom. "Is this room off-limits for us to use?"

"I own this yacht. Nothing is off-limits to you."

Her lips curled to the side. "Good." She walked over to the door and locked it.

What is she up to?

"I can't tell you how much I'm looking forward to this trip."

"Really?" he asked, his voice even deeper than normal.

"Really," she said, playing with the straps of her maxi dress. "Mainly because I've been looking for any excuse to get naked in front of you."

Josh swallowed. "For the record, you don't need a reason to get naked in front of me." He didn't even know what she had up her sleeve, but already he was semi-hard thinking about the possibilities.

Becca turned her back to him and slowly removed both straps from her shoulders. Her dress fell to the ground revealing a red lace corset and matching lace thong. Josh didn't even try to stifle his groan as his eyes roamed hungrily over her body in the vixen lingerie.

Becca turned her head over her left shoulder. "Did I mess up your tour?"

Josh didn't even answer. He had other business to attend to. The rest of the tour could wait.

Chapter 16

"We're here, sleeping beauty."

Becca opened her eyes and was immediately hypnotized by his ocean-blue irises. Once her surroundings started to come into focus, she remembered kissing Josh, having sex with Josh, then falling asleep with Josh.

Becca yawned and sat up in the bed, pulling the sheet with her. "Guess we never did make it to those master bedrooms."

"Nope, but we can head up there now before we get off the yacht and check out the island."

"Let's do that." Becca stood to get dressed and froze.

"Are you going to watch me get dressed?"

"That was the plan."

She laughed. "Well, can you not?"

"My staff's all on the first floor and all I have to do

is notify them to remain scarce and they will. And both masters are on the part of the third floor that we haven't gone to, so you can stay wrapped in the sheet and I'll lead you upstairs to the master."

Becca looked down at the sheet then at her discarded clothes on the floor. She really didn't want to get redressed. "Okay, let's head to the master."

They exited the guest bedroom and walked to a narrow spiral staircase that Becca hadn't noticed before. His yacht was so grand; she was sure it would take days for her to see everything.

Once they were on the third floor, Josh led her to the part of the floor that she hadn't yet seen. A set of double doors sat on each side of the aisle. Josh placed his hand on a device outside of one of the doors. He stepped aside when it slid open.

"It only opens to your handprint?"

He picked up her hand, punched in a code, then placed her hand over the device.

"Accepted," the device said when a light turned green.

"Nope," Josh said. "It opens for my handprint and yours." He led her inside. "Welcome to my humble abode."

Becca was in awe when she took in the polished mahogany floors and the glass door leading to a covered outside deck with two teak chairs. She turned to the left and noticed a huge California king bed with two glass night tables.

She laughed. "No wonder you stretch out in my queen bed. You're used to living like a king."

"I love your bed."

"Why do you love my bed when you have this?"

Josh pulled her to him, her sheet flittering to her feet. "I love your bed because you're usually in it." He gave her a quick kiss.

Becca probably would have kept on kissing him had he not continued the tour of the master. He opened the sliding door to the bathroom.

"Wow." She beelined to the bathroom and froze when she stood in front of two steps leading into the gray square bathtub in the middle of the floor. "I don't even have the words to describe how beautiful this is."

She glanced to her left and admired the standing shower with multiple nozzles and a bench. *No doubt we'll have some good times in there.* To her right, there were his-and-hers sinks. Becca walked to the sinks and opened the closed door to find a toilet and a bidet. *Unbelievable.*

"Josh, why haven't you brought me up here until now? It's gorgeous."

"No reason in particular. Since I live on the water, usually we're closer to your place, so it's just easier to go there after our dates."

Becca didn't exactly buy that excuse but she didn't want to talk about it at the moment. She'd much rather stay in her Josh-induced bubble a little more.

"The other master is similar to this one, but slightly different in style. How about we get dressed and I'll show you the island."

"Sounds like a plan."

Thirty minutes later, she'd taken a quick shower and put on her teal sundress that was simple yet sexy with a plunging neckline. Josh had blindfolded her so that she couldn't see anything.

"Almost there," he said. "I'm going to lift you in my arms for this next part."

Despite his warning, Becca yelped when she felt herself being lifted off the ground. A couple minutes later, she was back on her feet.

"Okay, here we are." He removed her blindfold. "Welcome to Purity Haven Island."

Becca's hands flew to her mouth at the beauty before her. From the angle they were standing, Becca felt as though she could see the entire small island.

"It's beautiful! Is this a private island?"

"It is," Josh said with a smile. "I've owned it for about four years now, but it's still a work in progress."

Becca's eyes flew to Josh just as he pushed his sunglasses on top of his head. "You own Purity Haven?"

"Yes, I do. Soul's First Kiss and I have been coming here for four years, but as of a couple months ago, I finally got the grounds just the way I wanted them. Each section of the island is called something different. I eventually want to name the main lodge and each of the villas I had built, but I haven't found the right names yet."

Becca was in complete awe of the sight before her as well as the man staring back at her. *He owns an island! He's gorgeous, sexy, smart, talented, comes from a good family, is hardworking and...he owns his own freaking island!*

Her heart was racing a mile a minute at the news. Becca was never the type of woman to be overly impressed by money, but even she had to admit that this was pretty damn amazing.

"Josh, I don't know what to say." She stood on her tiptoes to hug him, overcome with emotion. "I'm so proud of you and what you've accomplished at the age of thirty-five. You are truly amazing and I don't want you to think I'm one of those women who only get impressed by wealth, because I am far from that."

"I know that about you, Becca." He hugged her back just as tightly. "It still means a lot to hear you say those words." They hugged for a few more minutes before Josh offered to show her around.

Lush greenery and beautiful tropical flowers grew everywhere she looked on the island. It was obvious that Josh had invested a lot of money into this property.

"I spent the better part of three years going back and forth from the States and Nassau to Purity Haven, planting, building, getting everything exactly how I wanted it. My brothers helped a lot. Sebastian's construction company had an entire team dedicated to this island and all of us pitched in to help build the main lodges and villas. When I initially purchased the island, it was nothing but untouched terrain. Honestly, I'm surprised we got it done in the short amount of time that we did."

The main wooden lodge was just as stunning on the inside as it was on the outside. As soon as she stepped through the door, she noticed the large wooden fans on the ceiling and the beige Spanish tile on the floor. The wicker furniture in the main area had posh beige cushions and in the center of the dining area was an elongated wooden table that would easily seat twenty people. Becca would bet money that it was custom made.

"The main lodge is the common area. Here we have the main kitchen, dining room, main living room, two full bathrooms and an entertainment room. The villas are each equipped with a bedroom, bathroom, kitchenette and living room."

"How many villas do you have?"

"Four standard villas and two premium villas. I figured if my brothers, mom and I had family vacations here, we wouldn't want to stay with each other."

Becca touched the wooden table, appreciating its beauty. "Is the plan for you to rent out these spaces when they aren't being used by family?"

"Yes, eventually. They're luxury accommodations, so I want to be certain they're priced accordingly. And since you can only get to the island by boat, I built the docking pier to make that commute from the main island easier."

"That makes sense. Will there be a staff here 24/7?"

"There will be when it's up and running. For right now, I have five people who check on the island daily. Of the five, two are living here full-time since I still have a couple construction projects in the works. While we're here, I'm paying my yacht staff double to assist with the island, as well."

"If the main house looks this good, I can't wait to see how the villas look."

Josh reached for her hand. "I'll show you my favorite villa. The view from that one is the reason I purchased this island in the first place."

Becca placed her hand in his, trying to will away the thoughts that were floating around in her mind. Being with Josh felt so perfect. So natural. So…right. *Careful, Becca…you could fall hard for a man like Josh.*

The question of the day was: Had she already fallen?

Josh observed Becca as the warm breeze caught ahold of her dress as she stood on the balcony of his favorite villa. She was holding her arms in a way that either meant she had a chill from the breeze or was overwhelmed by everything she was learning about him. Given that the air was warm, he figured it was the latter.

"Are you okay?" he asked, wrapping his arms around her from behind. She leaned her head into his chest.

"I'm fine. Just taking in all the beauty. It truly is a sight to behold."

She was right. No matter how many times he came here, he was captivated by its beauty. This villa felt more like a hideaway in the lush tropical jungle. It sat higher than anything else on the property with the exception of the mountain. The gracefully bowing trees outside of the balcony added a sense of privacy while never taking away from the view.

"I could stand here forever," Becca said as she turned into his arms.

"Me too." He kissed the side of her neck right before she lowered herself to her knees.

"Can anyone see us up here?"

Josh shook his head. "Everyone is on the yacht or at the main lodge. Even if they weren't, they couldn't see us up here."

"Good," Becca said, tugging down his khakis. "Because I've been wanting to do something for a *very* long time and I don't think I can wait any longer."

He knew what she planned to do the minute he saw that mischievous look in her eyes. However, knowing and experiencing were two different things. She slipped him out of his boxers and covered him with her warm mouth before he could even form a reply.

"Oh shit." He grabbed ahold of the wooden balcony rail as her tongue got to work. Typically, he was slightly more poetic with his words, but currently the only words shooting through his mind were either dirty or expletives, because Becca's tongue licking up and down his shaft felt too good for words.

"How many times have you imagined me like this, with my tongue wrapped around your dick?" she asked in between licks. "I'm surprised you're holding on to that rail instead of threading your wicked fingers through my curly hair."

And she's talking dirty, too? It was official. Josh was going to die on the spot from all the pleasure coursing through his body. He took one hand and ran it through her hair while the other continued to help him maintain his balance.

Josh saw movement in the corner of his eye and noticed it was one of the landscapers he'd recently hired. It was a man who'd recently retired and sold his landscaping business, but decided that he still needed something to do. He wasn't part of the regular daily crew and only came to the island once a month, but him being here meant the other commuters had arrived on the island.

"Becca?"

"Hmm?" She didn't stop, but instead added fondling him to the mix.

Oh crap. "Becca, baby. There's someone down below. At the angle he's at, he may be able to see us."

Becca looked up at him, her lips slightly swollen and glistening in the sunlight.

"Did you hear what I said?"

"I heard you."

Josh looked down at Becca's hands that were still stroking him.

"Joshua, is that you?"

Josh glanced down at the landscaper. "Hello, Mr. Colton. Yes, it's me."

"Hey, son. Nice to see you again. The place looks better from the last time I was here."

Josh wasn't sure if it was because Becca was on her knees, if the tree was angled just right to block her or if Mr. Colton just couldn't see that well, but it was obvious that the older gentlemen hadn't seen her.

"Nice to see you too, Mr. Colton. I didn't know you all would be here today."

"There was a storm last week, so we decided to come today. Didn't Lidia email you?"

Josh tried to think. "Yes, I do remember getting something about it."

"Good." Mr. Colton started walking away and then looked back up at Josh. "By the way, the yacht is looking nice, too. Did you get a new paint job?"

What the hell? Please tell me he isn't trying to start a conversation at a time like this. Josh looked at Becca and gave her a look that begged her to release him. Instead of heeding his plea, she covered him with her mouth again.

"Did you hear me, Joshua?"

Josh looked back down at Mr. Colton. "No, sir, I didn't get another paint job."

"Well, when was your last one? I heard it's important to keep up the paint on those fancy yachts."

Josh closed his eyes to block out Mr. Colton as he rattled on about the yacht. It wasn't too hard to block him out since Becca was zapping all his focus anyway. She was moving her mouth in an even faster rhythm than she had before and the sensations were so strong, he felt her tongue and lips on every part of his body even though she was focused on one part.

"Well, I'll see you later, Joshua. A couple members of your crew said you brought a woman with you this time. Can't wait to meet her." With that, Mr. Colton finally walked away.

As soon as he was out of eyesight, Josh leaned even more on the railing, unable to stand at the onslaught of Becca's mouth.

"Becca, I'm close," he warned. At least, he hoped he was warning her. He couldn't be sure since the words in his head didn't seem to match what he was hearing in his ears.

He said her name a couple more times, but it was no use. He exploded harder than he ever had, needing to use the railing to keep from falling to his knees.

She sucked him dry like a woman dying of thirst and Josh wasn't sure he'd ever felt pleasure quite like this before. It was the type of pleasure that made a man think there wasn't anything in the world he couldn't accomplish. Becca's lips gave him hope while at the same time draining his body of the energy needed to function like a proper human being.

"I can't believe you did that with Mr. Colton right there," he said when he was finally able to find his voice. He pulled up his boxers and khakis just in case Mr. Colton returned.

Becca smirked. "Oh, come on, Josh. I'm sure your staff has probably seen worse. You were never almost caught with any other women you brought here?"

Josh stopped what he was doing. "I've never brought another woman here."

Becca searched his eyes. "Never?"

"Nope," he said, shaking his head. "I've also never shown a woman who wasn't in my family my entire yacht before. Any woman who has ever stepped foot on Soul's First Kiss didn't make it past the first level."

At her stunned expression, Josh kissed her cheek and led her out of the villa. "Come on. Let's introduce you to the others."

Chapter 17

"This is amazing," Becca said for what was probably the five hundredth time since they'd arrived on the island a couple days ago. Between the beautiful land, Josh's staff and the way Josh had been treating her during their trip, she was on cloud nine.

They still hadn't talked about their relationship, but things had been going so well that Becca hadn't wanted to bring it up. She'd never been the type to need labels and Josh was treating her better than any so-called boyfriend ever had. *And you're the only woman he's ever brought here...* She still hadn't figured that one out.

They were leaving the island later that night and Becca really didn't want to leave. On Purity Haven, she felt like anything was possible. The island had a way of making any problems back home seem minimal.

"Check that out," Josh said, pointing to a tropical

bird in the sky that was swooping down to get a fish from the water. They were canoeing in what Josh had called Tranquility River, which was basically a stream of water from the ocean that had been carved through the land to form a canal.

"Don't be nervous, but we'll be in slight darkness for a short while as we go through this cave."

"Okay." As promised, they were only in the darkness for a couple minutes. When they came out on the other side, the vision took Becca's breath away.

"I call this area Tranquility Cove. Not too creative, but it fits."

"It's perfect." Becca looked on either side of the intimate cove and noticed the same lush greenery and tropical flowers that were everywhere on the island.

Josh hopped out of the canoe when it hit the sand and pulled it onto shore. Becca immediately looked at the brilliant blue sky when she stepped out of the canoe. That, combined with the aqua waters and colorful flora, made this entire section a hidden paradise. She smiled at Josh, who was already watching her intently.

"I knew you'd love it." He grabbed her hand. "You'll love this even more." She followed him to a small body of water.

"Can you tell what it is?" he asked. She shook her head. "It's a natural pool, created from the river and terrain combined. When the tide rises, most of the beach sand, as well as this particular area, get covered by water, which fills this hole. It's only about four feet deep, but with the natural minerals, it's like a cooler version of a hot spring."

Becca dipped her hand in the water. "You're right, it's warm, but not too hot."

"Sure is. Want to get in?"

"Of course I do." Becca removed her tank and jean shorts so that she was only in her white-and-black bikini. Josh took off his T-shirt and tossed his sunglasses on top of it. In his swim trunks, the man looked as if he'd just stepped out of a catalog.

"You surprise me, Becca," Josh said once they were both submerged in the warm water and leaning against the rocks.

"How so?"

"Take now for example. I thought you would have asked me more questions about why the water was so warm before you got in."

Becca thought about Josh's comment. He was right. There was a time when she would have never agreed to get into a pool of warm water without solid scientific evidence backing what Josh had told her.

"I could say the same about you. From all those articles I read, I thought you were such a playboy and ladies' man. Yet I'm the first woman you've ever taken here before."

Josh grinned before leaning his head on a soft part of the terrain. "There's a reason for that."

Becca squinted her eyes. "And what reason might that be?"

Josh glanced into the sky before meeting her gaze again. "Remember how I told you I was close to my dad's father before he passed away?"

"Yes, I remember."

"Well, my mom's parents are still living. Unlike my dad's side of the family, we were never close to my mom's parents growing up. Her father, in particular."

"I take it you still aren't close."

"Forget close. My grandfather and I don't even speak. He won't even acknowledge he has grandkids."

"Why wouldn't he acknowledge you and your brothers?"

Josh sat up a little straighter. "Because in order to acknowledge us, he'd have to acknowledge my mother, and he wrote her off the minute she decided that she didn't want to follow the path he'd laid out for her, and instead wanted to marry the mechanic she'd fallen in love with."

Becca nodded her head in understanding. "Your father."

"Yup. I meant what I said. My father was one of the most hardworking men I've known, but no matter how hard he worked, or the fact that he went from a mechanic to owning several shops across Florida, my mother's father always considered my dad beneath her and her family. And the man who took his baby girl from her Louisiana roots."

"But I've talked to your mom and I've never heard two people sound more in love than she and your dad were."

"I agree, and I grew up in a very loving home, but I watched my dad bend over backward to make his father-in-law happy, only to die knowing that he never did accomplish it. My mom came from money and my father was never welcome. Even after he passed, my mom went to her father to try to make amends because apparently, it's what my father had always wanted. Even then, that jerk refused to speak to her and I had to sit there and watch her hurt over a situation that never should have been an issue in the first place."

Becca could see anger in Josh's eyes. "You went to

him, didn't you? You went to your grandfather after you became a millionaire?"

"I did."

"But it didn't make a difference?"

"Not a damn bit."

"That's ridiculous. You're a millionaire now, making a name for yourself. You were invited to join a prestigious organization. Yet it's still not good enough for him?"

"Nope, not even close. And to top it all off, he's a member of one of Louisiana's Prescott George chapters. But since he disowned my family, according to the organization we're not related and I will never be a legacy. Which is fine with me. I don't need his last name, nor do I want it. My father was a DeLong. His father was a DeLong, and I'm building the DeLong brand without the assistance of my maternal grandparents."

Becca waded to Josh's side of the pool, stopping in front of him. "Josh, the DeLong name would be a great one no matter if you were a millionaire or not, because it's yours and it belongs to you and your brothers, who will pass it down for generations. Never allow anyone to define you based on their own biases. The saddest part about your situation with your grandfather is that he missed the opportunity to get to know a remarkable daughter, four charismatic grandsons and an amazing son-in-law. He lost so much more having never had the privilege of getting to know you."

The crease in his forehead eased. He pulled her closer to him. "Have I told you how amazingly brilliant you are?" He kissed one side of her neck before kissing the other.

"Not in those exact words." She giggled when he

hit her ticklish spot behind her ear. She slipped her hand into his swim trunks to get him to stop. His eyes darkened.

"You shouldn't have done that, Becca."

She nipped at his bottom lip. "Why not? What are you going to do about it?" Taunting Josh was slowly becoming her favorite pastime.

Without warning, he untied her bikini bottom and top in about three seconds flat. At her gasp, he captured her lips with his as his fingers found her sweet spot. Taking her cue from Josh, Becca untied his trunks until they were loose enough to pull off.

Becca tossed her head back in gratification as his fingers went to work, prepping her for what was soon to come. She smiled at the sound of paper ripping as Josh protected them both. *Is he ever not prepared?* Not only was Josh an attentive lover, but he was a skilled lover. She didn't have to wonder if he was on top of things when it came to sex or question if he knew how to please her. With Josh, it was guaranteed pleasure.

Instead of dwelling on all the questions she still needed to ask him, she banished all thoughts from her mind as she slowly eased him into her core inch by inch.

"Becca, are you okay?"

Becca looked up from the blank screen on her phone to her sister, Allison. "Yes, I'm fine. I was just thinking about something."

Allison frowned. "You've been daydreaming all night. How long are you going to make me wait before you give me details on your trip with Josh?"

"Let's finish helping Mom with the table first."

Becca had been home for four days and all she could

think about was Josh. The trip had been nothing short of amazing, until he received an urgent business call when they were an hour away from Miami. Although Josh had tried to act like the call hadn't put a damper on the last hour of their ride home, she could tell his mind had been preoccupied.

When they finally docked, he told her he had to go to LA for a day. One day had turned into several and even though he video chatted with her every night and texted her throughout the day, Becca had to face the harsh reality that she'd gotten accustomed to seeing Josh in person on a daily basis.

"Okay, let's eat," Becca's mother said.

Becca sat down next to her sister, wishing that her brother-in-law hadn't taken her nieces and nephew to Georgia to visit his parents. She needed a buffer...or four. Her father was no help. After living in a house with so many women for over twenty years, her father, who sat at the head of the table, had learned to block them all out.

"It's so nice having both my daughters here," Patricia Wright said. "The only thing that would have made tonight better would have been Becca inviting Joshua DeLong to dinner."

"Mom, I already told you—he's out of town and I haven't even seen him since we got back from vacation."

"How was it by the way?" Allison asked. "You still haven't said."

Becca glared at Allison. "It was great."

Their mother frowned. "Great? That's it? What did you do? Where did he take you?"

Why did I agree to come tonight? This was a lose-lose situation. If she told them the truth, they would be even more in love with Josh. If she lied to them, they would know, because her mom and Allison always knew when she was lying.

"It was…" Her voice trailed off as she tried to think of something she could tell them that would do minimal damage.

"Well?" her mother asked. "Tell us something."

"Patricia, leave Becca alone," her father said. "If she wants to tell you and Allison what happened, she'll tell you at her own pace."

Patricia's eyes grew wide as they always did when she was about to be dramatic. "Well, excuse me for wanting to know how my daughter's trip went with a man who may be my son-in-law one day."

"Mom, it's not even like that."

"How would I know what it's like?" her mother asked. "You talk to your sister, but you won't even talk to me, your own mother."

The doorbell rang and Becca's father was all too eager to answer it.

"Do you realize how old your father and I are? Don't you want us to be able to enjoy our grandchildren?"

"Of course I do, Mom." Becca shuffled her food around on her plate. The truth was, she wanted to tell them all about the trip, but she couldn't exactly lie and say she and Joshua were in a relationship. Yes, she knew that they liked one another and the time they'd spent together so far had been nothing short of amazing, but Becca didn't know what would happen after the gala next month. Would she and Josh still see each other? Did they need to categorize what they were or was she satisfied with keeping things the same? Was she even in a situation to ask him to define what they were?

She decided to be as honest as she could. "Josh and I had a great trip, but I don't even know where we stand with one another. He's an amazing man and we work really well together. He's nothing like I thought he would be, yet somehow, he's turned out to be so much more than I ever imagined. If I let myself get wrapped up in everything, I will fall for him harder than I have ever fallen for any man in my entire life. The only reason I won't gush about Josh is because I don't want to get your hopes up by telling you how amazing the trip was, just to realize that it didn't mean as much to him as it did to me."

"It did mean a lot."

Becca turned toward the entryway of her parents' dining room and gripped the table to keep from bolting out of her seat. "What are you doing here?"

Josh's eyes stared intently at her. "My flight just landed an hour ago and when I tried to call you, it went straight to voice mail."

"My phone died."

"Oh, that explains it." He glanced at her mom and sister as if he were debating whether he should continue. "I called the office and Haley answered. When I told her I was looking for you, she gave me your parents' address. I hope that's okay."

"It's fine." Becca sat up straighter in her seat. "You just surprised me, that's all."

"I guess it was a bit impulsive." Josh glanced at her lips and his gaze lingered there for a while. Out of nervousness, Becca licked her lips.

"I like impulsive." *At least, I do now.*

Even though her family was in the room with them, Becca couldn't take her eyes off Josh. It was as if they were two magnets drawn to each other by force.

"For the record," Josh said, "our trip to Purity Haven meant a lot to me, too. Probably much more than you realize."

She smiled at his statement before it dawned on her that he probably heard a lot more of her conversation with her mom and sister than she'd expected.

"Purity Haven?" Allison asked before Becca could go into full freak-out mode over the fact that she'd basically admitted that she was falling for Josh and he'd practically been standing a few feet away when she'd said it.

"It's my private island," Josh said. "It's located in the Bahamas and that's where I took Becca last week."

Becca chanced a glance at her mom and sister, who were surprisingly well-behaved considering the fact that they'd been asking her about Josh for weeks and suddenly he'd appeared in the doorway. *Maybe they finally understand that I can muscle through my own love life without their input.*

"I've always wanted to plan one of my daughter's weddings on an island. Since Allison is already married, that just leaves Becca. Lucky for me, her future husband already owns an island."

Spoke too soon! "Mom, I can't believe you said that. It's not even like that."

"Says who? You just admitted that you're falling for the man and here he is in my dining room drooling over you like a love-sick puppy. You both are too cute for your own good. Josh, how about you take a seat and make yourself a plate. I need all the details about the island for future planning purposes."

As Josh stepped farther into the room, Becca had only one coherent thought.

Kill me now.

Chapter 18

"Josh, this is a serious accusation."

Josh glanced over at the other men who were seated at a table in the corner of the bar waiting for him and Daniel to join them. They'd called this meeting to solidify their alliance against the current Prescott George president and to form a strategy to oust Ashton Rollins.

"Look, I know it's serious, man," Josh said to Daniel. "That's why I pulled you away from the other guys. I wanted to talk to you about it separately."

Toward the end of his trip with Becca, Josh had received some incriminating information about Ashton Rollins. While he was in LA on business, he'd called his contact to get the details and had been shocked at what had been discovered.

"Daniel, do you understand what I'm saying? According to my sources, after college, Ashton was driving the car when his girlfriend Mia died in the wreck. Somehow, the authorities reported that Mia was behind the wheel and under the influence. There's no police record of Ashton being the one behind the wheel."

"I heard you the first time," Daniel said, a little louder than before. "But you don't understand. I went to college with Mia and Ashton. Mia wasn't just a friend. Until Angela, I always considered Mia the love of my life. It took me years to get over what happened and now you're telling me that it's possible that Ashton killed Mia? It's too much, man."

The emotion that Josh heard in Daniel's voice gave him pause. However, knowing that Daniel was so close to Mia made it even more imperative that Daniel understand the bigger picture.

"Daniel, my heart goes out to you, man, but if you put your relationships with Mia and Ashton aside, you'd see this the way that I do. You know the Rollins family. They ooze money—enough to bribe anyone if they had to. What if the police were paid for their silence, and this entire time Mia has been made out to be irresponsible and a drunk, when in actuality, Ashton was the one responsible? Instead, he gets off scot-free. Since you knew both of them in college, I know I'm not saying anything you haven't already thought about before."

The torn look on Daniel's face proved to Josh that he was right. Daniel was a smart man and there was no doubt this scenario had run through his head before.

Daniel sighed. "Listen, I'm still on the fence. You just laid all this on me, so let's tell the fellas we will reschedule the meeting, and then you and I can talk about it later this week."

Josh already knew what he wanted to do, but he understood why Daniel needed time. "Okay, let's do that."

"Are you sure everything is okay?" Becca asked for the third time. She hated sounding like a broken record, but from the moment she met Josh on his yacht that night, she'd known something was wrong.

"I'm fine," he said with a forced smile.

Becca squinted her eyes, not believing him for one second.

"I guess LA drained me," he finally said. "A couple of months ago I had to let go key members of the management staff for a tech company. We finally came to an agreement during my last visit, but I think I just need to reboot. Want to sit out on the top deck with me?"

"Sure."

Becca followed Josh to the top deck just as streaks of lightning sliced across the sky followed by the sound of thunder. "Are you sure you want to stay out here? Looks like it'll rain soon."

When she looked at Josh, she noticed tension leave his shoulders and the sly smile he usually wore return.

"What's wrong, Becca? Scared of a little rain?"

She jumped at the rumbling in the sky combined with Josh tickling her sides. His sudden mood swing caught her off guard, but she welcomed the teasing side of him. Before long, Josh was playfully chasing her around the top deck as the first drops began to fall from the sky.

"Too bad you don't want to go inside." Becca pushed Josh onto a teak lounger with a thick black cushion and white pillows. "Guess you'll never get to see what I have on underneath this skirt."

Becca was still wearing her black pencil skirt and white blouse that she'd worn to work that day, but underneath, she was sporting a treat that she was sure Josh would appreciate.

"Any reason why you can't show me out here?"

"For starters, it's raining and I don't want to get my hair wet."

"Your hair looks amazing when it gets wet."

"Well, the temperature will also drop if it rains."

Josh ran his finger down her exposed leg. "We generate enough heat to keep us warm."

As always, even the simplest touch from him was enough to warm her entire body. As the rain grew heavier, Becca pushed away from Josh with an entirely new plan in mind. Feeling his calculating eyes watching her every more, Becca slowly unbuttoned her blouse before tossing it to the side. Even in the darkness, she could feel his eyes boring a hole through her black satin bra, causing her nipples to peak.

Next, she stood right in front of him with her back turned and eased her pencil skirt down her hips and thighs, giving him the perfect view of her backside. Once she was only in her lingerie, Becca unbuttoned Josh's shirt, then unzipped his pants. When he stood to remove them completely, she pushed him back down on the lounger and wagged a finger at him.

The rain was completely soaking them both, but now Becca was too anxious about what was yet to come to go inside. She eased herself on top of Josh, grinning when his eyes widened at the skin-on-skin contact.

"Are these…" He slid his finger to her center. "Crotchless?"

Becca nodded, ripped the condom packet with her teeth and slid it over his shaft.

"The fact that you're so prepared is sexy as hell," Josh said in a strained voice. Becca lifted her body again and eased herself on top of him.

Josh let out a throaty groan as every inch of him went deep into her core. He whispered words near her ear. Out of all the things she'd grown to enjoy about the way Josh made love to her, the uninhibited way he spoke during intimacy brought her desire to new heights.

It didn't take long for them to begin moving in their own special rhythm. With each thrust, Becca felt her body widen even more to accommodate Josh. Mentally, they connected on so many levels, but physically, they were in a category all their own.

Before long, their lustful moans drowned out the roaring sound of the sky as they made love to one another in a way that could only be described as unrestrained passion.

After they showered, they lay in Josh's grand king bed wearing soft white robes, each caught up in their own thoughts.

"I needed this," Josh said, breaking the silence.

"I know you did." Becca hadn't liked seeing him so stressed out when she'd arrived earlier. Especially since she was hoping they could talk.

"How was your day?" she asked.

"It didn't go exactly how I'd planned."

"More issues with one of your companies?"

Josh played with her still-damp hair. "No, it's something with the Moguls. Do you remember meeting the president of our chapter, Ashton Rollins?"

"Yes, I believe he introduced himself right before our presentation." Becca also recalled how tense Josh had gotten when Ashton had approached them.

"Well, right after college, Ashton's girlfriend was killed in a car accident and it was reported that she was under the influence while driving. But I've heard from a source that Ashton was actually the one driving, which means the Rollins family could have paid off the police for their silence."

Becca shot up from the bed. "So he's possibly responsible for her death, yet it's been hidden this entire time?"

"That's what I suspect based on what my source says. Maybe I haven't told you everything, but a few of the Moguls and I are trying to transform Prescott George by bringing them out of the Dark Ages and into the twenty-first century. Daniel and I are leading this initiative and the first line of business is to dethrone Ashton. Revealing this news will only help our case."

"But there's a possibility that it's not true, right?"

"Right, but there's an even bigger possibility that it is."

Becca's mind was reeling. "If the Moguls are rocked with this scandal, what would this mean for the foundation?"

"The foundation doesn't have anything to do with this."

"Not directly, but indirectly we do. If Ashton is relieved of his position and a criminal investigation takes place, there's no way that Prescott George's charitable activities will continue. Everything will probably be put on hold. The Aunt Penny Foundation needs the donations from the gala as well as future support from the organization."

"You're getting ahead of yourself," Josh said, sitting upright, as well. "The foundation will be fine."

Becca shook her head. "You don't know that. Besides, you don't even know if the information is true, yet you're willing to risk destroying a man's life?"

She suddenly recalled the conversation they'd had in Purity Haven. "Is this truly about clearing his late girlfriend's reputation and gaining control of Prescott George to better the organization? Or is this some attempt to win the support of your mother's father by whatever means necessary?"

Josh got out of bed and walked to the window. Becca could tell he was angry, but she was angry, too.

"How dare you take something that personal and turn it against me?" he said when he turned to face her.

"I'm trying to make you see reason," Becca said, getting out of the bed. "I don't want you to be so blinded by the way your grandfather treated you and your family that you assume ruining the life of another man and taking his place in the organization is going to make you feel better and give you the acknowledgment and power you deserve."

"This isn't about power," Josh said. "This is about the truth. In today's society, a poor man who commits a crime will get sentenced to years in prison. Yet if a man who comes from money pays off the right people, he gets off free of any charges."

"That's assuming that he did it," Becca exclaimed. "I agree that the system isn't fair. But you are not God and I'm only trying to get you to ask yourself some serious questions, to consider how this news will affect everyone around you. This is not as simple as turning Ashton in. There's a strong possibility that something like this could open up a can of worms and hurt more Prescott George members than just Ashton. What does that mean for the other members like you? Or organizations that benefit from the Moguls?"

Josh was already shaking his head. "I may be a millionaire, but I know I'm not above the law. For years, people with money haven't been held accountable for their actions and haven't had to face the same consequences as those from the lower and middle classes. It sickens me to see how society treats people differently based on their social standing."

"What about people like me?" Becca yelled. "My family is from money and so are a lot of their friends. I can only speak for my parents, but they didn't raise my sister and me to believe we're above the law. Nor did they raise us to treat people differently based on social standing."

"Your family is an exception, not the average upper-class family."

"Wow," Becca said, shaking her head. "The air must be thick on that high horse you've placed yourself on. So screw Ashton and the Rollinses. It doesn't matter who gets caught in the cross fire, right?"

Josh stiffened. "I've never kept the type of man I am a secret from you. You know what I do for a living and in my profession, blunt honesty is sometimes the only way someone can see what they have done wrong. I live an honest life and it isn't my fault if others don't."

"You know what's funny?" Becca walked closer to him. "I grew up in an upper-class family and I spend night and day trying to help less fortunate students get to college so that they can get the same kind of education that I never questioned I would have. But I'm not special. I don't think I belong on a pedestal. I don't think anyone who does charity work should get a daily badge of honor. Yet here you are—a boy from humble beginnings who grew up to be a millionaire in a cutthroat industry, who day in and day out wants an award for going through what he had to face in life. And yet, at the end of the day, according to you, I'm the one who feels entitled." She held his gaze. "But you're the one throwing a whole lot of entitlement around."

"Like I said, you knew who I was from the beginning."

The look of determination in his eyes made Becca stop arguing. He wasn't looking at her. He was looking through her. Of course, she'd always known what Josh did for a living, but seeing him blatantly disregard how his decisions may affect the foundation and other charities was beyond her comprehension. *You always knew there was a chance he'd be like the others.*

"I have to go," she said, throwing back on her wet clothes as quickly as possible. "I'm not sure when I'll be back."

Becca walked to her car without looking back. Once again, she'd allowed a man to get close enough to her to cause her to take her eyes off the prize. In this case, the prize was solidifying enough support for the foundation so that she and Haley wouldn't have to worry year after year that they'd be shut down.

Becca waited until she was in the confines of her car to release the shaky breath she'd been holding. "Good job, Becca. Way to pick another winner."

You will not cry over this man. You will not cry over this man.

Becca was still chanting the words to herself as she tried to call Haley.

Chapter 19

"Do you want to play another round?" Logan asked.

Josh glanced at the time. After three hours of playing video games at Logan's house, Josh was finally starting to see the reasoning behind his own frustration.

"Naw, I think I've played enough games for one night." When Josh had told Logan about his argument with Becca, it hadn't taken long for his brother to tell him that he was in the wrong. Seeing her leave his yacht earlier that night so hurt and disappointed by him had crushed him more than he'd ever thought possible.

"She's the one, isn't she?" Logan asked, breaking into his thoughts.

"Yes, she is. In the back of my mind, I always knew she was. But the idea has really slapped me in the face these last couple weeks. And tonight just proved it even more. She put me in my place, and although she left upset and ready to cut my tongue out of my mouth, I still can't help but see my future when I look at her."

"I figured," Logan said with a laugh. "Otherwise you wouldn't still be sitting here looking sorry for yourself."

"I don't look that bad."

Logan laughed. "Yes, you do, man. I don't think I've ever seen you like this. But we all think Becca is perfect for you and, secretly, I don't think Mom could ever stop talking to Becca even if the two of you did break up."

"I wouldn't want them to stop talking. Mom's elated when she talks to Becca. But Becca just has that effect on people. She's the type of woman who brings folks from different walks of life together in the same room in perfect harmony. You should have seen her at the animal shelter. All the families who came in loved her."

"Dude." Logan put up his hand to stop him. "We've talked about Becca for hours. And you keep repeating the same stories."

Josh smiled sheepishly. "Sorry. I guess she's really on my mind."

"Which is why you should be at her place and not mine."

"What am I supposed to say?"

Logan stood from his chair and pretended to knock on a fake door. Then he dropped down on his knees and clasped his hands in a praying position. "Hi, my name is Joshua DeLong and I'm a huge idiot. Is there any way you can find it in your heart to forgive me?"

"Bro, I can't say that to her. I said some terrible things and now in hindsight, I realize she was right about everything she said about me. I don't want to lose her, but I'm sure we can think of something better to say than that."

"Fine." Logan sat back down on the couch. "Let's brainstorm."

"She said you can go on up."

"Thank you," Becca said to the doorman of Aunt Penny's Miami Beach apartment. When Becca exited the elevator to Aunt Penny's floor, the older woman was already waiting in the doorway.

"Aunt Penny, you shouldn't be walking around."

"How else am I supposed to answer the door? Besides, my doctor said I should be fine as long as I take my blood pressure medicine and eat healthy. You know I'm a tough old bird."

"I know," Becca said as she hugged Aunt Penny. Becca followed her into the apartment. "Thank you for letting me visit you so late. Haley wasn't answering the phone and I really need someone to talk to."

"No worries, sweetie. What's wrong?"

Becca told Aunt Penny the entire story. After she finished, she expected Aunt Penny to read her the riot act and tell her to kick Josh to the curb, but the woman did neither.

"Well, do you have any advice?"

Aunt Penny smiled. "My dear, there are two sides to every story, so although I'm sure you believe you were right, you probably haven't considered Josh's side in this matter."

"He could possibly be condemning an innocent man and he doesn't care who he hurts in the process."

"I don't think Josh would ever purposely hurt

you," Aunt Penny said. "The man I saw at the hospital couldn't get enough of you."

Becca smiled for the first time in hours. "But what about his determination to dethrone Ashton?"

Aunt Penny shrugged. "What about it? Josh could easily run Prescott George, and whether you understand his view or not, he has had to fight hard to get where he is today and there are many people who will always hope that he fails. The power struggle between old money and new money has been going on for centuries. Josh will continuously have to prove himself worthy of being a millionaire. You should understand that. You've spent years trying to prove that you didn't need to be someone's wife to succeed."

Becca put her head down. "I never thought about it that way."

"Becca, I'm not taking sides. But you may not be one-hundred-percent right and Josh may not be one-hundred-percent wrong. Life is never black-and-white. It's filled with a lot of gray, and the gray stuff is the hardest to work through sometimes. You love this man. I can see it in your eyes. I can see his love for you in his, as well. You have nothing to gain by walking away. I've always told you that avoiding a problem is not solving one. Don't let your stubbornness stand in the way of your happiness."

Becca reflected on Aunt Penny's advice, seeing the fault in her actions for the first time tonight. She didn't want to admit that Josh could be right. What was even more shocking was her revelation that she actually liked the ruthless, take-no-prisoners side of him. It was sexy even.

"I think I need to talk to Josh. I'll head back to my condo and figure out what I'm going to say."

Aunt Penny smiled. "That's my girl. I plan on going to the gala next month and your wedding next year, so you and Josh better work this out."

"Working this out doesn't mean we're getting married."

Aunt Penny patted her arm. "Yes, it does, dear."

Becca tried to think of different ways to apologize to Josh the entire way home. She came up with only one. *I'm sorry for not considering how you felt. I thought I saw life in color only to realize I see life in black and white, and I failed to consider all shades of gray.*

"If you say that, he won't know what you're talking about," she said to herself. She parked her car and walked to her building. At the sight of Josh standing in front of her complex, her steps faltered but she managed to maintain her balance.

The minute she reached him, he dropped to his knees and put his hands up, as if in prayer.

"Hi, my name is Joshua DeLong and I'm a huge idiot. Is there any way you can find it in your heart to forgive me?"

Becca blinked a few times before bursting out into laughter. "Oh my goodness, I needed that laugh. I've been trying to figure out ways to apologize to you all night."

"Me too," Josh said. "I'm sorry for what I said and how I said it. You mean so much to me and our relationship is too important to let this argument come between us."

"I agree," Becca said. She tugged on Josh's arm until he stood up. "I was only viewing the situation through my eyes when I should have been viewing the situation through your eyes, as well. I'm so used to being right that I sometimes don't know how to accept that I'm wrong." She had to admit that was a much better apology than what she'd rehearsed in the car.

"I'm no longer going to ambush Ashton with the information I was given. I'm going to do some more research and then I'll approach him man-to-man and see if his story has any merit. Prescott George is a brotherhood and despite the fact that Ashton and I don't get along, I can't do this to a fellow brother."

Becca searched his eyes. "Even if it means you'll probably never become president of Prescott George?"

"You've changed me. I used to think winning was everything, but now I realize there are more important things than winning." Josh took Becca's hands in his. "Don't get me wrong, winning is still very important to me, but not when it means losing the woman I love."

If Josh hadn't been holding Becca's hands, she was sure she would have stumbled to the ground. "You love me?"

Josh's lips grazed her cheek. "More than I ever thought I could love anyone."

Becca grinned as she leaned her forehead to his. "I love you, too…but I thought I might be in this alone."

Josh smiled wider than Becca had ever seen him smile before. "For the record, my entire family loves you too, so I may have some competition."

Becca laughed. "Yeah, well, I'm pretty sure my mom and sister love you more than they love me, so we're even."

For a couple minutes, neither of them said anything. When Josh did speak, his voice was serious. "I knew from the minute I met you that you would impact my life in ways I hadn't yet figured out. You challenge me. You motivate me. You understand me. Your support and love mean more to me than you'll ever know. Now that I've found the woman who's perfect for me, I can't imagine my life without you in it."

Becca was filled with so much emotion, she couldn't string together the words to respond to such a beautiful sentiment.

"I know," Josh said, pulling her closer. "I know." When his lips touched hers, Becca poured all her heart and soul into their passionate kiss.

Epilogue

It had been a week since Josh professed his love to Becca, but it felt like it had been so much longer. He hadn't wasted any time asking her to move into his yacht, but being the independent woman she was, Becca had insisted on Josh giving his request some time. She didn't want to impose on his personal space so quickly. But if he had his way, she'd never go a day without knowing he thought no space was good space when it didn't include Becca Wright.

He was glad that he'd listened to Becca and thought more about the situation with Ashton. When he'd contacted Daniel and told him about his plans to not ambush Ashton, but instead get more information and approach him man-to-man, Daniel had seemed relieved—and impressed—by the decision. Josh was still skeptical about Ashton, but overall he was confident he was making the right choice.

"So, are you finally going to tell me the meaning behind 'Soul's First Kiss'?" Becca asked, breaking his thoughts.

Josh grinned. "This yacht was my first huge purchase after my business took off. I had always thought my first big purchase would be a house for my mom, but she wanted to remain in the house that she and my father raised us in, so instead we just did renovations, updated the bathroom and kitchen, that sort of thing. My family thought I was crazy for wanting to live on the water, but I knew what I wanted. When I saw this beauty, it spoke to my soul."

Becca kissed him on the cheek. "That's beautiful, baby."

A goofy grin erupted on his face. He loved how she called him "baby." In fact, there were so many things that he loved about Becca. And the list seemed to get longer every day.

"What about Purity Haven? Does that name mean something?"

"It does. My dad used to always say that no one can live forever, but if we find a place that truly makes us happy, we will always have our own personal haven of purity. To my dad, being happy was a sure way to extend your life and I guess calling the island Purity Haven was a way for my dad to live on… A way for me to communicate with him since he is constantly an inspiration in every facet of my life even though he's no longer here."

It didn't surprise him to see so much emotion in Becca's eyes. "That's beautiful," she said in a soft voice. "And it fits the island perfectly."

"Thank you." Josh studied her eyes, finally understanding why he could never figure out the perfect names for the properties on the island: because it was always meant for Becca to choose those names. She just didn't know it yet. "Why don't you relax? I'll be right back."

"Okay."

Josh left Becca lying out in the sun by the pool on the second deck.

When Josh got to the gate, his package was right on time.

"Thanks, bro." Josh dabbed fists with Logan.

"No problem, man. Good luck!"

"Thanks." Even though Josh kept trying to calm his nerves, he still couldn't do so. But with each step he took toward the deck where Becca was relaxing, he felt more calm.

Becca turned to him when she heard movement behind her.

"DeLong, what is in that big box you're holding?"

Josh held the box out to her as he walked over. "Why don't you open it and see?"

The minute she opened the box, she squealed at the small bundle of brown fur that jumped out at her.

"Oh my God, a puppy?"

"Not just any puppy," Josh said.

"Wait… Is this a Lab and golden retriever mix? You got a combination of the dogs we each grew up with?"

"Yes, I did." Josh loved to hear the excitement in her voice. "I got you something else, too. Check out his name."

Becca looked up at Josh with laughter in her eyes. "This is too perfect. You named him Bugatti."

"Had to," Josh said with a smile. "I fell in love with

you the minute you yelled out the name of my favorite car."

Becca stood up and gave him a big hug, careful not to squish the puppy.

"Just so you know, Bugatti belongs to both of us," he said. "I'm already earmarking certain places for him on the ship."

"I can't wait to visit him all the time."

"You won't have to visit him because you'll be living on the yacht with us."

Becca frowned. "Josh, we've been through this. You just told me you love me a week ago. Are you sure you want me to move in so fast?"

Josh nodded to the dog collar. "Why don't you open that pouch that's on Bugatti's collar."

Becca looked at him with skepticism, but she untied the pouch. When she opened it and looked inside, Josh gave her credit for not dropping the puppy.

Josh took Bugatti in his arms and dropped to one knee, pulling the ginormous engagement ring completely out of the pouch. He captured Becca's left hand as her right flew to her mouth.

"Becca Wright, I know it may seem like our love has progressed fairly quickly. But for me, it feels like I've waited my entire life for you. When two people share a love like ours, it doesn't take long for one to realize that a future without the other isn't a future worth living. There are so many amazing qualities that you possess and I'd never want you to be anyone but yourself. I fell in love with the woman you were. The woman you are. And the woman you will be. You'd be standing here for hours if I listed all the reasons why I love you and why I can't wait to start our future together. So I'll try to make this question as simple as possible… Becca Wright, will you be my first mate for life?"

By now, Becca was crying and even then, Josh still thought she looked adorable. "Yes, Joshua DeLong. I'll marry you."

Josh barely had time to place the ring on her finger and give her a kiss before their families erupted in applause.

Becca turned to find the Wrights and DeLongs approaching them on the deck. She faced Josh. "How in the world did you pull off getting everyone on the yacht without me noticing?"

"That would be my doing," Logan said, taking a bow.

Josh pulled Becca in for another kiss until Bugatti got jealous and started showering them with his own kisses, his little pink tongue furiously licking one then the other.

"What do you want me to do about this one?" Becca and Josh turned to Sebastian, who was holding another puppy. This one was all black.

Becca raised an eyebrow as she turned to Josh. "Two puppies?"

Josh shrugged his shoulders. "They're sister and brother. I didn't want to split them apart."

Becca took the other puppy from Sebastian. "Hello, Maserati," she said as she scratched her ears.

"How did you know what I named her?"

"Because I know you, and those are the two cars that you own that you picked me up in."

Josh winked at his brothers since they hadn't thought Becca would understand his naming conventions.

Becca walked back over to Josh and gave him a kiss

that wasn't interrupted by the puppies. "Just so you know, I draw the line at kids."

"What do you mean?" Josh asked.

"It means that although I think it's adorable that we're naming our dogs after luxury cars, we can't name our kids after cars, too. I have to draw the line with them."

Josh laughed so loud both puppies started licking his face. "Baby, the thought never even crossed my mind."

* * * * *

He'd noticed her the moment she walked in, and it was clear,
even in an eye-popping black gown, that she was there as
more than an invited guest. He could tell by the way her
gaze covertly scanned the room, noted the exits and followed at a discreet distance from the vice president that she
was part of his security detail—secret service. He had an
image of a .22 strapped to her inner thigh.

Unlike many highbrow gatherings of politicos and the
like that were too reserved for Rafe's taste, a Lawson party
was the real deal. Full of loud laughter, louder conversations
and the music to go with it. So of course he had to get
particularly close to talk to her.

He gave her time to assess the layout before he approached.
He came alongside her. "Can I get you anything?"

She turned cinnamon-brown eyes on him, fanned by long, curved lashes. Her smile was practiced, distant, but Rafe didn't miss the rapid beat of her pulse in the dip of her throat that belied her cool exterior. Her sleek right brow rose in question as she took him in with one long glance.

"Clearly you're not one of the waitstaff," she said with a hint of amusement in her voice.

"Rafe Lawson."

Her eyes widened for a split second. "Oh, the scandalous one."

He pressed his hand to his chest dramatically. "Guilty as charged, cher, but I have perfectly reasonable explanations for everything."

Her eyes sparkled when the light hit them. "I'm sure you do, Mr. Lawson."

"So what can I get for you that won't interfere with you being on duty?"

She tensed ever so slightly.

"Trust me. I've grown up in this life. I can spot secret service a mile away. Although I must admit that you bring class to the dark suits and sunglasses."

She glanced past him to where her colleague stood near the vice president. In one fluid motion she gave a barely imperceptible lift of her chin, a quick scan of the room and said, "Nice to meet you," as she made a move to leave.

He held her bare arm. "Tell me your name," he commanded almost in her ear. He inhaled her, felt the slight shiver that gripped her.

"Avery."

Rafe released her and followed the dangerously low-cut back of her dress with his gaze until she was out of sight.

Don't miss SURRENDER TO ME
by Donna Hill, available August 2017
wherever Harlequin® Kimani Romance™
books and ebooks are sold.

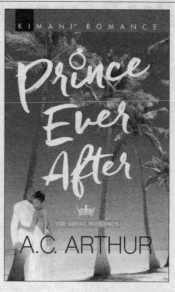

A love for all time

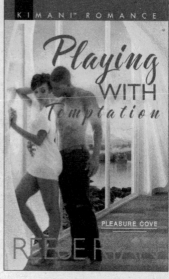
REESE RYAN

Playing
WITH
Temptation

Pro football player Nate Johnston is in need of a miracle when a viral video threatens to derail his career. After breaking his heart, repairing his career is the least media consultant Kendra Williams could do. As passion smolders between them, will a jealous ex sabotage their second chance?

PLEASURE COVE

Available July 2017!

080471805